The Black Angels

Cal Clark

Acknowledgments

I'm happy to acknowledge the many debts I owe for all the help I have received with this book. Foremost, two skilled authors, Jim Buford and Marian Carcache, generously mentored me. They read and commented upon the text, leading to many improvements, large and small, and also introduced me to the complex world of publishing fiction. I literally can't believe the time, effort, and support that they contributed to my effort to write a murder mystery. Phil and Deb Harris provided extensive help and encouragement in making the book a reality. In addition, Jim Buford and Cortez Lawrence read the text to ensure that I didn't make any major errors about law enforcement, and Jan Widell patiently answered my many questions about psychiatric hospitals and nursing. I also received encouragement, support, and important suggests from my wife, Janet Clark. Other comments that affected the book came from Al and Linda Cuzan and from my three daughters, Emily Federico, Ellen Clark, and Evelyn Benavides. Period books that I consulted included *Abnormal Psychology and Modern Life* by James Coleman, *Danvers State: Memoirs of a Nurse in the Asylum* by Angelina Szot and Barbara Stillwell, *Human Problems of a State Mental Hospital* by Ivan Belknap, *Mental Hospital* by Alfred Stanton and Morris Schwartz, *Psychiatric Nursing* by Katharine Steele, *Psychiatry in Nursing* by Raymond Headlee and Bonnie Wells Corey, *The Snake Pit* by Mary Jane Ward, and *The Shame of the States* by Albert Deutsch. I also surfed the web and can recommend googling "psychiatric nurse humor" whenever you're out of sorts.

Chapter 1 ~ The Black Angels

Carol Mason was a light sleeper but the ring of the telephone jolted her awake without grogginess or fond memories of delightful dreams. She reached for the lamp on her bedside table, snapped it on, the clock displayed 1:18. Her first thought was that little good could come of a call at that time of the morning. She rose, reached the telephone in the alcove between her bedroom and sitting room, and answered it.

"Miss Mason, it's Clem."

"Hi Clem, it must be a major problem. Has a patient died, escaped, or gone on a rampage?"

"No ma'am, we need to go out to get a patient. I can come by to get you in ten minutes. Do you have your rain gear? It's pouring."

"I have my boots, but my slicker and rubber helmet are in my office."

"I'll bring them. Can you be ready in ten minutes?"

"Make it fifteen, please."

The innocuous exchange put Carol on alert. That the Director of Nursing and the Chief Attendant would be sent to pick up a patient at any time was extraordinary. Being pulled from her bed implied an emergency that surpassed anything that had occurred during her three years at Elm Hill Psychiatric Hospital for Women. Moreover, Clem's calling her *Miss Mason*, and especially *ma'am*, indicated that somebody powerful, and probably not friendly to either of them, was listening to his end of the conversation.

Carol turned toward the maple bureau at the foot of her bed, a family heirloom that her parents had given her two years ago to celebrate her appointment as Director of Nursing. This represented a major promotion from a shift supervisor and jumped her over the Nurse Managers for Elm Hill's ten wards. It also gave her a two-room suite, plus private bathroom, rather than the small dormitory room without a bath that she had had before in Brackman Hall, a dormitory for the unmarried nurses, nursing students and, more recently, nurses' aides. The suite also came with its own telephone, a luxury that Carol shared with the three Nurse Managers who lived in Brackman. She no longer had to use the public wall telephones where younger nurses giggled as they talked to their boyfriends and grimaced when their mothers warned them about "bad boys."

Pulling out underwear, white stockings, and a clean pair of white gloves, she briefly considered whether it was worth the bother to struggle into her girdle. However, she quickly decided that, especially since she didn't know where she was going or what she would be doing, she wanted to look as professional as possible. She got her nurse's uniform, her cap, and picked up her large purse as she left her bedroom and retrieved her rubber knee boots from the entryway closet.

Carol's room was at the back of the first floor, but she had a relatively short walk to the entryway. Looking out through the window at the downpour, she was grateful that Clem was bringing her a heavy slicker and rain helmet. Almost immediately, the hospital's ambulance arrived. She opened the door to admit Clem whose rainwear was already glistening from even the short walk to the steps of the porch. He smiled and held out the raincoat and hat to Carol.

"You know, Carol, maybe the storm is appropriate. It's turned us into black angels," Clem said as he nodded toward the hall mirror reflecting the two garbed in black rain gear. "We're giving someone help, or at least the chance not to ride Old Sparky, but unlike real angels we're certainly not taking her to the good place."

Carol, still not totally awake, gave a little smirk. They dashed to the shelter of the ambulance and once inside Carol asked what was happening.

"Dr. Carson called me at home a little after midnight and told me to meet him at the hospital. When I got there he said that there had been a gruesome murder. Judge Adams was blown apart by his daughter Carrie with a shotgun at their mansion on River Ridge and that the police wanted the killer to be committed for a psychiatric evaluation. He had already signed committal papers and wanted the two of us to transport the patient here because the case is very sensitive."

"Thanks for the summary. I knew that somebody nasty like Carson must be around when you called me 'ma'am' and that something pretty serious had happened, unlike when you call me at midnight to get a poor drunken nurse out of jail."

Clem laughed and said, "Some cops do like to go after our girls, don't they? The attendants are a lot worse, but they don't get arrested unless they cause significant damage to somebody or something. Gladys deserved a night in the drunk tank for puking and peeing on the steps of City Hall. But poor Emma, hauled in just because a nasty old sergeant claimed she was staggering. I don't think that the girl even drinks."

Clem turned off the through-street they were on to a side road without street lights. "Believe it or not, this goes up the Ridge and brings us out behind the big houses. Doc Carson told me to take it and that we'd be met at a back gate into the mansion's gardens. It's the third house after the road has a left bend just after the crest."

The road curved away from the houses through a wood, leading them in less than a mile to the foot of a ridge that rose about two hundred feet through dense foliage that looked impenetrable through the heavy rain and almost total darkness. They drove in silence for several minutes as Clem squinted into the gusting downpour to navigate the four switchbacks up the hill. Once they reached the top, the road dropped slightly and then swung sharply to the left to parallel the ridge top to the left and the back walls of the properties that faced River Ridge Road to the right.

"Darn it, Carol. Can you tell where the backyards are separated? I thought there would be lights and a welcoming committee."

"I know we've passed one. I think that gate up there might be number three."

Chapter 2 ~ The Suspect

Clem rolled the ambulance to a slow stop as a slight figure moved from the sparse shelter of a gate through the ten-foot wall, waved its arms, and tapped on Carol's window and motioning her to open the door. Carol did and then slid to the middle of the seat. The interior light briefly showed a young woman's face in the square opening of her rain hood. It seemed to Carol that she looked on edge in a way that was unexpected for an officer presumably conducting a murder investigation. Indeed, nervousness, if not a little fear, was reflected in her voice.

"Turn off the car and the lights. We need to go quickly. The Medical Examiner is supposed to be here at three. We need to get Carrie out of here and to the hospital before that because she'll be taken to jail as soon as he's finished. That gives us less than an hour."

Carol's response was strong and stern, "Who are you? Are you a policewoman? Aren't you investigating a crime? We're not here to fight the police."

"I'm Emily Jenkins. I'm a meter maid not an officer, but I was ordered to help Officer Harker. I don't know what's going on. Someone high up wants her committed and not prosecuted, but they evidently don't want the people investigating here to know until she's locked up in the hospital. Please, hurry. You're Miss Mason, aren't you? They're a little afraid of you."

"Carol, whatever have you done to frighten the police?" Clem asked.

"Rescuing Emma, as you might well guess, Clem. Let's relive old times later, though. Emily's right, we need to hurry, not try to make sense out of this crazy situation."

Her words seemed to calm Emily who said, "We can't risk a flashlight. Walk straight behind me. There's a little light filtering back from the front of the house. I'll take you up the servants' stairway at the rear. Leave your rainwear on and don't worry about making a mess or causing a problem for the investigators. We're a long way from the murder site so no one should be looking at the stairs or the second-floor back bedrooms for clues."

Emily opened her door and stepped out. Clem then reached back, pulled a green canvas duffle bag forward, and whispered to Carol as she started to slide toward the door that Emily had left open, "Sarah Harker is a mean one, but nobody's ever accused her of being close to the top brass."

Within a couple of minutes Emily had guided them to Carrie's bedroom. When they entered, a uniformed policewoman half turned from a comfortable armchair that had been positioned near the bed. She appeared to be about thirty, a little over a half decade younger than Carol, with a strong face, hard eyes, and a light brown ponytail.

Her low voice was authoritative, crisp, and to the point. "I'm Officer Harker. Are you Mason? Do you have the committal papers? What's he doing here? Don't you know we'll have to undress her?"

Carol didn't hide her lack of deference. "Clem is our Chief Attendant who brought the committal papers. More importantly, I need his help in getting her restrained. It also looks like he'll have to carry her out. What have you done to her? What did you give her?"

The question turned everyone's attention to the girl on the bed who seemed to be in her late teens. Her right hand was handcuffed to the headboard, but the restraint was superfluous because she was in a nearly catatonic state with glazed open eyes and no movement. She had an oval face and dark brown hair that might once have been pretty but was now matted and disheveled. She was wearing a green dress that was spattered with blood from below the waist to the neckline.

Clem and Carol had already shed their raincoats, while Emily remained frozen by the increasingly angry hisses of the other two women. Clem pulled a plastic folder from the top of the duffle bag and handed it to the policewoman. "Here's your copy of the committal order, ma'am. It's signed by both Judge Welch and Doctor Carson. Don't worry about me peeking at what I shouldn't. I'll step outside until she's ready for the jacket."

Sarah seemed momentarily relieved and mollified. "Thank heaven. Without the committal papers Detective Perkins would slap me in the cell they have reserved for her." Carol, who had already grabbed a pair of rubber gloves from Clem's duffle bag, turned businesslike and said, "I don't know what's going on, but we need to cooperate. Clem's outside already. I assume you need to take all her clothes for evidence."

Without speaking, the two women got the girl undressed. As Sarah arranged the clothing as evidence at the bottom of the bed, Carol returned to the duffle bag for thick cloth diapers.

"Please, Emily, come here and make yourself useful. That's a good girl. Raise her legs so we can put diaper cream on her bottom. Okay, good. Now hold her there, while I get the double diapers under her and pinned. Good girl." It was unclear, though, whether the last was directed to Emily or Carrie. "Now, let's get her sitting on the side of the bed again. Good. Pull those rubber pants up over her knees. Good girl. Okay, I'll hold her up now. Get the pants up over the diaper. Make sure the diaper is completely covered. She'll be in it all night so she's sure to be soaked. Okay, sit her down again and get Clem."

While Emily went to the door, Carol picked up a cord belt, slipped it through the loops at the top of Carrie's pants and secured it with a small padlock at the back. By this time, Clem had returned and extracted a heavy white canvas strait jacket from the duffle bag.

"Here ma'am, keep her sitting. I'll get her arms in the front. Now, let's get her standing between the two of us. Okay, now you've got the back straps fastened, here are the sleeves. I've got her elbows positioned so that the jacket won't be too tight." Carol then pulled the two sleeves together and buckled them behind Carrie's back to get the jacket fully secured.

They refrained from the smiles they would have normally shared for a job efficiently done and then looked up to see Sarah and Emily looking at them wide-eyed, probably for different reasons. Carol smiled at the meter maid and said, "One last chore Emily. Please hold her up while we get her dressed for the storm." Clem emptied the once bulging duffle bag by extracting a set of rainwear for Carrie.

Carol looked at the policewoman again. "We need to know what was used for sedating her. Was it sodium amytal? It must be something powerful. The doctors certainly won't want a drug interaction."

"I'm sorry, but I don't know. I'm just a cop. She was like this when I got here. Can I ask a big favor? Could you take Emily home? Nobody knows she's here. It might be a good idea to keep it that way. There'll be enough of a stink when they find out you've carted that damn murderess off."

Clem and Carol were already back in their rainwear. Clem easily picked up Carrie while Carol turned to the now obviously disconcerted meter maid. "Come Emily," she said, "you're already dressed for the weather. You can lead us back to the gate and the ambulance. Goodbye, Sarah. We made a good if not congenial team. We're in and out in less than twenty minutes. We should be back at the hospital by a few minutes before three."

The policewoman seemed a little uncertain about how to respond to the use of her first name, but in the end nodded nervously and replied, "We had to. I don't think you understand any more than I do."

On that ambiguity, the three retraced their steps. Just as they reached the ambulance, the darkness was momentarily broken by a huge flash of nearby lighting. Once they started the trip back to Elm Hill, they remained silent until Clem reached the bottom where the road widened, not wanting to break his concentration on driving, or perhaps just trying to assimilate their strange experience. Then Carol exhaled a little more loudly than she had intended. "We've made good time. We're okay if Emily is right that we have until 3:30 or a little later before anyone knows that Carrie's been taken away. We should be back at Elm Hill well before that. Emily, you obviously know more than you've been able to tell us so far. How did you get here? What were you told?"

"I was getting ready for bed about 11:30 last night when my mom came up and told me that I had a phone call. When I picked it up, a stern voice said, 'Miss Jenkins, you must go on duty now. You'll be assisting officers in a murder investigation. You've never done anything like this, but unfortunately you're the best available woman we can get tonight.

"He told me to get into my uniform and dress for the storm because I would be out in it several times. In ten minutes a police car would pull up on the street in front of our house. I should tell my parents just that I had to go on duty because of a shortage of women officers. When the patrol car pulled up, I ran out through the rain and followed his instructions to get into the back seat on the passenger's side. As I was pulling the door shut, I suddenly saw that this was one of the cruisers where half the back seat was shut off from the front and the other half by wire mesh. I couldn't stop from slamming the door and gave a little shriek as I realized I was locked in a cage. When I looked over, the driver looked pretty big. He was wearing the same type of rainwear like we are so I couldn't see what he looked like. He didn't sound like the man on the phone, but he had a commanding voice like the other guy. He said I was in the cage because I couldn't be allowed to see his face. He told me that he was taking me to a mansion on River Ridge Road where Judge Adams' crazy daughter had just murdered him. I had to help Officer Harker tend to the prisoner.

"I wasn't happy to have to report to Officer Harker, though. She scares the rest of us women, even the ones she doesn't outrank, like you do the nurses. She was pretty tense when I got there, but she didn't seem to be upset with me. We talked for ten to fifteen minutes. Then we pretty much sat in silence for about an hour until her radio beeped three times, which was the signal for me to come get you."

"Thanks for the run down, Emily. From what you say, somebody must have been keeping close tabs on our arrival, which suggests that they've got their eyes on us now. That's amazing and a little scary. At least we've reached the hospital. Now, Carrie will enter custodial care for the criminally insane under regular procedures."

By now they had been let through the gates and were circling to the large garage at the back of hospital. An attendant came to meet them with a wheelchair for Carrie. Carol asked Clem to take Emily home and then nap at Elm Hill before meeting her in her office at 6:30. As they waited for Clem to return from helping trundle Carrie to the Violent Ward, Emily turned to Carol. "Please, ma'am, if it's okay to ask, who is Clem? You two seem to act very differently toward each other when nobody else is there."

"Certainly, it's fine to ask. Tonight, as I said earlier, you're one of us. You're also perceptive. I'm the Director of Nursing, so I organize and supervise all the nurses and nurses' aides at Elm Hill. Clem is the Chief Attendant who supervises all of them. In organizational terms, I have a much higher position. We also move in very different social spheres. Yet, both of us work hard, care about helping our patients, and cooperate much more than people in our positions normally do. We've become close friends and respect each other greatly, but we can't show it in public."

She smiled and then continued, "Do you want to hear about why the matrons are frightened of me?" When Emily nodded, Carol went on. "One evening seven months ago three of our nurses were at a bus stop downtown, giggling after a funny movie and probably after flirting with some boys. A police car stopped. It was a desk sergeant going in for the 11 o'clock shift. He claimed that one of them, Emma Hughes, was drunk and disorderly. The girls claimed that all they had was soda and popcorn at the movie. In any event, he handcuffed her and took her away.

"Julie and Nancy, the other two girls, were so angry and scared that they called me directly. I made a telephone call, got a hospital car, and arrived at the police station about half an hour after the arrest. I walked into the station just as the desk sergeant's telephone was ringing. Beyond him, I saw poor Emma handcuffed to a bench and crying, evidently waiting to be taken to the cells. I rushed over and started to comfort her when the door behind me creaked open. Almost immediately I was grabbed by both arms, pulled away from her, and spun around to face a large muscular matron, red in the face with rage. 'Put your hands on your head. I'm arresting you for interfering with a prisoner.' Before I could reply, the sergeant screamed, 'No, Dora, No. We have to release the nurse. Apologize or we'll be in real trouble.' The matron went from rage to fear in a couple of seconds, un-cuffed Emma, and then said in a whisper, 'I'm sorry, I didn't understand.' On our way home, Emma confessed that she had flirted with the sergeant several times because she liked policemen, but then she found out that he had a wife and three children and became afraid of what he wanted to do to her."

Emily could hardly conceive of anyone who could intimidate Dora "the Bully" Butler. "Please, ma'am, who did you call? Who could make those two back down?"

"It's best you don't know who it was, but it's somebody who can convince powerful people to right wrongs, as long as it's not too costly. As I told you earlier, I don't have any access myself to politicians or the police brass."

Chapter 3 ~ Undercurrents

Carol decided that three hours of sleep was better than none and used a small room with a cot in the administrative suite on the first floor for a rest. She entered her office, neatly uniformed, capped, and made up at 6:15. An oversized desk with two empty trays and a blotter on its top dominated the back of the room. The front was divided between a round table with five chairs around it on one side and two padded comfortable armchairs with a small stand between them on the other. She immediately had the switchboard operator connect her to Ward 6.

"Hello, Emma. Is everything all right on the ward? Mrs. Simmons is wandering again? No, don't restrain her. Just put her back to bed gently. Could you please fill an insulated coffee carafe and bring it to my office? You're very good with paperwork, so, I hoped that you might help me if I run into trouble with the admissions forms for a patient whom we brought in last night. You can tell the attendants to call if any trouble erupts before the 7:00 shift comes on duty."

She dashed up to the Admissions suite on the second floor, got several forms from the counter, stopped briefly to skim them, and returned to her office. Next, she got three large mugs and a sugar bowl from the wardrobe, placed them on the stand between the armchairs, and went to the entrance to the administrative suite to find Emma who was tapping at the door. Clem was only a few steps behind her. Emma was Carol's height but about ten years younger with a much slighter build that made Carol a little jealous of her. When they reached her office, she indicated the two armchairs for her colleagues and then rolled over her comfortable office chair behind the desk to join them.

"Be comfortable. Emma, please pour the coffee. There's a big sugar bowl. I would guess that the coffee needs substantial sweetening at the end of a shift."

The three took several long contemplative sips, then Emma asked, "I'm so glad that I can help after what you did for me. If you give me the forms, I can start making a draft."

Carol smiled. "Emma, thanks for being willing to help. I don't need much help with paperwork, though. I've gone over the forms and I understand them. My one question now is what should I do since both Judge Welch and Doctor Carson signed the committal papers?"

"Judge Welch would be the initiator, while Dr. Carson would be her psychiatrist in the hospital."

"Thank you. That's pretty simple. I do have one other thing. According to Nurse Jeanie Watson, you're fantastic at helping new patients adjust to the hospital. We just brought in a patient a few hours ago who needs all the help that she can get. Last night Judge Adams was murdered, supposedly by his daughter Carrie. Instead having her arrested, Judge Welch committed her for a psychiatric evaluation.

"We brought her here in a strait jacket, but there were three very disturbing things. First, she had been grossly over sedated long before we got there and even before the policewoman, who had her in custody, arrived. Perhaps it was incompetence, but it really looked to me like somebody didn't want Carrie saying anything for a substantial amount of time. Second, the kick of the shotgun should have bruised her shoulder pretty badly, but her right shoulder was totally unmarked. Third, the dress that Carrie was wearing was soaked with blood that presumably spattered when the Judge was shotgunned at close range. When we removed her clothing, though, I saw that the bloodstains stopped suddenly at the top of the dress. There was no splatter above the dress. It looked like someone else had worn the dress when they killed the judge and then transferred it to Carrie's sedated body."

Clem responded with awe in his voice, "I knew that you're a super Director of Nursing, but I had no idea that you were a super detective as well."

Carol laughed heartily, while Emma looked bewildered. "Nursing involves a lot of detecting. You just have to use your brain and look for symptoms. That's pretty much the same, isn't it? In any event, Clem, can you talk to your friends among the Negro cops and ask them to look for evidence beneath the surface?"

"Certainly, the investigation will be so big that several will have to be involved. In addition, Detective Perkins may turn something up. He's smart, honest, and a hard worker. That's why he lost his wife and will never be the Chief of Detectives. Is there anything else?"

"No, make a few calls from outside the hospital, go home and collapse. Give my best to Ella."

After Clem left, Carol held out her cup to Emma. "Let's have a second round. There's something that made me think of you as we were bringing Carrie in. We had a meter maid with us who had been dragooned into the scheme for reasons that aren't obvious. She said that some of the police, especially the jail matrons, are scared of me and asked why. I told her about rescuing you. Really, she seemed shocked when I brought Dora the Bully into the story."

"I'm glad they're scared. I was so frightened and humiliated. I'd heard what she does to nurses, both us and the ones from Osloville Medical Center. I think she hates us because we're educated and professional. She's very rough in her strip searches and then locks them up with prostitutes, mocking them, and telling them that they need to learn what a real *profession* is."

Carol felt regret. Clearly, the five nurses who, unlike Emma, had been incarcerated before their release over the last two years should have been given more comforting than reprimanding. Despite the coffee, she suddenly felt exhausted from the busy night.

"Are you done Emma? Leave the cup, Gwen does a wonderful job cleaning up after me. Let's go see if you can do anything to help poor Carrie acclimate to the Violent Ward. It's after 7:00 so they should have her fixed up unless she's still unconscious. I would assume that she'd be the first one treated by the new shift."

"What would you like me to do with Miss Adams? I can tell her about hospital procedures and try to get her calmed down, but I have no idea what to say about the murder. She must be very frightened. I'm a little afraid that I could make things worse."

"Unfortunately, that's a very good point, Emma. I think all we can do is reassure her that she's safe at Elm Hill and suggest that she should be very careful in talking to the police."

The women had to descend to the basement and then walk along a narrow, dingy corridor to the back of their building and a solid door marked, Violent Ward. Carol inserted one of her keys and opened the door into a short corridor with lockers along its walls and another heavy door at the end. When they opened the second door, the nurses were immediately confronted by a large attendant in blue coveralls who snapped without looking at them. "Who the hell are you? Everyone's checked in for this shift. Nobody else is allowed. How did you get a key? This is a highly secure ward. Miss Rayburn could have you dismissed."

Emma flinched and stepped backward, but Carol glared back at him. "I'm the Director of Nursing. Is your mind so slow that you don't remember who I am? I have authority to go anywhere in this hospital. I can have you fired. I'm here to see the patient that Chief Attendant Jones and I brought in last night. Where is she?"

"Cell 13," spat out the attendant.

Emma had never been in the Violent Ward, though she had heard wild rumors of what went on there. At this time in the morning, though, the solitary confinement of all the patients meant that there was little to see, unlike in her ward where there would be plenty of patient activity. Instead, they were walking down a corridor that was deserted except for the disgruntled attendant behind them. There were doors with oval observation windows about ten feet apart on either side. Carol, who seemed to be confident about where they were going, turned into a side corridor. When Emma followed she saw a tall nurses' aide exiting from a room about thirty feet away. She wore an aide's uniform, a white blouse and a white pinafore, but in addition she had on a black rubber apron and gloves, as well as a surgeon's mask and a white bathing cap. She started to turn toward them, stopped abruptly, swiveled in the other direction, and rushed toward the nurses' station where the hall dead ended.

"Miss Mason, why's she dressed so strangely?"

"Don't you talk to anyone who works here, Emma? Well, I guess they're a pretty self-contained lot. While it only happens every once in a while in our other wards, there are some patients here who regularly try to douse the staff with a full food plate or even their own wastes. The most junior nurses' aide gets stuck with handling them. On this shift, it's Amy Strong who is very sensitive about her beautiful hair and had a snit when she had to cut it to meet our uniform regulations. Her character, however, is far from beautiful. So, there're several people down here who laugh when she gets messed up. I'm worried, though, because I think that she came out of Number 13."

Indeed, the door from which Amy had exited was marked 13. Carol opened it with her key, stepped inside, and audibly gasped as she viewed Carrie. The girl was sitting on the bed still confined in her strait jacket. In addition, a short chain had been attached by two padlocks, one to a ring on the back of the jacket and one to a similar ring embedded in the wall to keep her in a sitting position. Her restraints had also been augmented by leather leg straps and a rubber gag. Carol turned back toward a stunned Emma. "Close the door. This is atrocious."

"Hello, I'm Carol Mason, the Director of Nursing. Do you know you're Carrie Adams?" The girl nodded yes. "Do you know you're in Elm Hill Psychiatric Hospital?" The girl didn't respond and looked uncertain. "Did you know your father was murdered last night?" At this, the girl shook her head "no" and began to sob. Carol dropped down beside her on the bed, held her with her left arm, and stroked her hair with her right hand. Then she whispered in her ear so softly that even Emma couldn't discern what she said, "Something bad is going on, Carrie. Whatever you know or don't know, just say that you don't remember anything until I tell you it's okay. Blink once if you can understand." Carrie blinked once. Carol rose and with Emma trailing after her left the cell and turned up the hallway in the direction that the nurses' aide had taken.

Chapter 4 ~ A Difference of Opinion

The hall ended in about thirty feet in a nurses' station. There was a nurse in her mid-40s sitting behind the counter who watched their approach warily. "Yes, Miss Mason? What is it? Is that Emma Hughes with you?"

"How are you, Jane? Are you in charge of the ward right now?"

"No, ma'am. Miss Rayburn came in with the seven o'clock shift because of the new patient."

"Then I need to see her. The treatment of Miss Adams is highly irregular."

"Please ma'am. We're just following the doctor's orders. I'll take you to Miss Rayburn immediately. She's very upset that you're interfering. Oh, ma'am, please, I don't mean to be disrespectful."

Jane, seemingly relieved that no scathing reprimand was directed toward her, smiled wanly, got up, came around the counter, and unlocked a door on the left marked "Nurse Manager." Carol, and after a questioning look at her superior, Emma followed her in. They entered a spacious anteroom lined with file cabinets around a vacant secretary's desk with an open door to a conference room on the left. Jane walked to the closed door on the right and knocked.

An unwelcoming voice bid them enter. June Rayburn, a stocky woman in her 50s with curly gray hair, sat behind her large desk, looking formidable in her white uniform. Jane turned to the left and Emma to the right, as both seemingly tried to fade back into the nice wooden bookshelves that spanned the front of the room. Carol stepped forward two paces and stood behind the two wooden chairs in front of the Nurse Manager's desk.

She commenced in a sweet voice that soon began shading into sarcasm, "I just stopped by to check on the patient that we brought to the Violent Ward last night because she was semi-comatose from over sedation. I was shocked when I saw what you had done to her. How often do you keep a patient straitjacketed in her room unless she's totally uncontrolled? She was sitting docilely so the heavy restraints don't seem justified. And the gag? Even if she screams, why gag her in her cell, which is pretty soundproof? I can't remember that being done when I worked here. Anyway, if she's in a gag, she must be supervised in case she starts to choke. You don't want to kill our most prominent patient, do you?"

"We're following Doctor Carson's orders. She's a homicidal maniac, the most dangerous patient we have. She blew apart the most decent judge in the county, just because he took her drugs away from her. She's a monster. What will the police think if we're letting her run around free when they come to question her?"

"I'm sorry. I'll check the new texts to catch up with what a 'monster' psychosis is."

Sarcasm was not the best strategy for mollifying Miss Rayburn.

"How dare you. Are you defying the doctors? And why did you bring that untrained nurse to my ward? She's your creature isn't she? You saved her from jail? When Nurse Lattimore was Director, a drunken nurse would have spent the next month on her hands and knees scrubbing toilets and bathroom floors."

"I brought Miss Hughes because of her excellent record for integrating new patients into ward life. As to her arrest, it was totally trumped up."

The two protagonists suddenly became aware of the sobbing behind them. Miss Rayburn reacted first, jumping from her chair and rushing to Emma. To the great surprise of a frightened Jane and an angry Carol, she embraced the girl.

"Emma, Emma. I'm so sorry. I'm so sorry. I didn't mean it. I know you're a good nurse. The whole hospital does. We're so proud of your outpatient clinic for abused wives and children. I know you're a good girl, too. We go to the same Church, I never should have said that. I knew it wasn't true."

Turning to Carol, she continued her apologies. "I'm sorry, Miss Mason. I'm upset because I've never been pushed around like this. This is the worst thing that's ever happened in the history of Elm Hill. It's unprecedented. The doctors have the authority to set the patients' treatment. We had to do what he said. But, you're certainly right. This is excessive. I'll contact Dr. Carson immediately and ask him to make his orders in line with hospital procedure. I'll let you know as soon as we talk. Jane, go remove Miss Adams' gag. Miss Mason is right. Gagging her is unjustified and dangerous. Amy may well have done that on her own."

Carol smiled, though not entirely sweetly and sincerely. "Thank you, June. I'm glad we could work things out. Please call my room when it's settled. After being up all night, I need to rest."

After leaving the office complex, Carol looked at Emma and briefly brushed her finger across her lips. When they were back on the first floor, Carol asked Emma to meet her by the front door in fifteen minutes so they could walk back to Brackman together. She then bolted up the stairs and a short way to the left along the corridor across the front of the hospital to Admissions. Two nurses sat behind the counter that ran across the front of the anteroom.

"Hello, Marlene. Hello, Cindy. Are you doing well today?"

Marlene responded somewhat tentatively, "We're fine, Miss Mason. Is there something wrong? I can't recall your coming in here since you became Nursing Director."

"I believe you're right, Marlene. There's no problem about Admissions, but I think you should do something extra for the new patient whom you'll be processing shortly. I would guess you've heard that Judge Adams was murdered last night and that his daughter was committed here for a psychiatric evaluation. Evidently, she shotgunned him.

"Clem Jones and I transported her here. She was almost comatose, presumably from some combination of over sedation and her own drug use. The police didn't do anything with her. Thus, you should take blood and urine samples and photograph her body. Make sure that you do a close-up of her right arm where the sedation was injected. I'm sure that Dr. Rydberg will ask the police if they need anything else, although there's such a time lag now that it might be hard to get much that will be of any value."

Marlene, relieved that she was not in trouble, agreeably offered that Lucy Sims, the hospital's head lab technician, could get the photographs developed and ready for the police by early afternoon.

Carol met Emma at the front door a few minutes later. Once they were on the walkway back to Brackman Hall, Emma almost burst out with her curiosity. "Please, ma'am. Why are they so mean? Why did you accept their claims that Carrie's a murderess after what you just told Clem and me? Why did you shush me? Did I do something wrong? Will Miss Rayburn and Doctor Carson get me in trouble? What can I do to help you?"

Carol stopped and patted her reassuringly first on the arm and then on the back. "Emma, Emma, so many questions. Let's hope I don't forget what they are before I finish answering. I didn't say anything about the fishy evidence for two reasons. First, we didn't have any friends in the room. So, trying to change their minds would have been futile. Second, we don't have much of an idea about what's happening. In a situation like that, we need to look innocent and dumb until we have a much better idea what we're facing. I should have warned you that you can't talk in the Violent Ward. They have microphones in the cells and voices carry more than you think in the corridors. Also, Lord knows where that sneak Amy Strong had got to. She must have run to Miss Rayburn as soon as she saw us."

"Should I try to see Miss Adams? I'd love to help you."

"No, stay away from this. There's danger somewhere, but you don't have to worry about getting in trouble. You were there with me and didn't do anything except take some undeserved abuse. In addition, it didn't sound like Miss Rayburn and Doctor Carson are on good terms about this. There's enough ill will so nobody should bother you if you stay away from Carrie. It's a pity. I thought that you might be able to help her and hoped that she might confide in you what happened, but for your own good as well as hers you need to stay away and show no interest in her whatsoever. Actually, I hate to say it, Miss Rayburn has a good point that bringing an outside nurse into the Violent Ward is somewhat problematic.

"However, if something comes up that doesn't involve Rayburn and her Violent Ward, I'll ask you for help right away. I have a bad feeling that that may happen. Earlier, when Clem saw us dressed in our rainwear, he called us Black Angels who care for people in unfortunate circumstances. Now you're wearing similar raingear, too, so welcome to the Black Angels. I am afraid that we're going to have to help Carrie and Elm Hill before long."

"Oh, ma'am. I feel so good that you trust me. I do have something to tell you. As we were walking away from the entrance into the Violent Ward, I'm pretty sure that I heard that nasty attendant mutter, 'Interfering bitches. We'll get you soon.' What does that mean?"

"He's obviously the resentful type, but that seems to be going overboard. The $64,000 question is whether there is a *we* that we need to worry about. When Miss Rayburn called Carrie a drug abuser, she showed that some nasty scheme is afoot. How could she have any idea about that? Thanks so much for telling me, but this is all the more reason for you to ignore everything about poor Carrie for now."

Carol soon reached her room, where a few more chores awaited her. A nurse with very neat feminine handwriting had taped a note to her door asking her to call Miss Rayburn immediately. Carol called the Violent Ward as soon as she removed her rainwear.

"Hello, June."

"Thanks for calling, Carol. I'm glad to report that Doctor Carson agrees with us. The patient will have to sleep in restraints, but during the day she won't be restrained in her cell. If she loses control of herself, she'll be packed, not strapped into a strait jacket. When she leaves her room for exercise or police interrogation, however, strong restraints will have to be applied because she's exceedingly dangerous to others and perhaps to herself. In particular, she must be placed in a strait jacket and leg restraints and, unless she is talking to the police or a doctor, gagged. Doctor Carson also agreed, furthermore, that a gag can only be imposed if she is accompanied by a staff member."

"That's good news, June. Thanks for taking care of it. I still think that the gagging is excessive, but you're right that she's probably the most notorious patient we've ever had. 'Better safe than sorry' sounds like a good adage." The two women then wished each other well in civil and not overtly insincere terms.

As soon as this conversation was over, Carol picked up the phone and asked the operator to connect her to her secretary, Gwen. "Hi, Gwen. Anything new come up? That's a blessing. I've been up all night with a horrendous case, as I'm sure you know if you've gone to the cafeteria to fill our coffee urn. Please cancel my meetings for the day. I'm about ready to collapse. One last thing. Could you please contact

Dr. Rydberg's office and ask whether he wants me to be available when the police come? Carrie should be ready for them by late afternoon. Thanks so much. You're wonderful."

Carol had time to get out of her uniform and girdle, but not to don her nightgown or brush her teeth when Gwen called back to say that Dr. Rydberg wanted her to come to his office at four to meet with Detective Perkins.

Chapter 5 ~ A Wonderful Invitation

My name is Andy Russell. It was the day after May Day, 1955, a Monday. Though nobody I knew had ever celebrated it, my spirits were dancing as if there were a May Pole right in front of Washington Hall at State University. Graduation was five weeks away. Moreover, I had already been awarded a research assistantship to work on my Master's degree in Psychology for the following year. The next month promised to be quite easy, at least in academic terms. Due to my heavy course loads in several previous semesters, I only needed to take 12 hours this semester. Six of them, in addition, were for my senior research project which I had turned in a week ago. Apparently, Dr. Calder, with whom I would be meeting later today, had been happy with it. Professor Metcalf, the other woman faculty member in the Psychology Department, had just stopped me on my way out of class. She smiled and told me that I should see Dr. Calder at 1:30 and that she had some very good news to give me. "You're going to have a wonderful summer, Andy. Dr. Calder's the one to tell you about it, though. I'm excited for you. In fact, I'm almost jealous."

Dr. Calder, who taught the Abnormal Psychology courses for the Psychology Department, was a thin woman in her mid-50s with dark hair that was turning gray. As far as I knew, she was a spinster, but from what I'd heard, women in academia often have to sacrifice their personal lives to get ahead professionally. Her face wasn't particularly pretty, but it often held a kindly expression. She seemed atypically warm and welcoming when I reached her office on the third floor of Washington. She began by praising my research paper and saying that it could be the first step toward a PhD dissertation. She then said that she would have the Department switch my assignment next year from helping a professor with our introductory course to working on a grant that she had received to study psychiatric institutions in the Midwest, along with two PhD students.

It was hard to give her an adequate response. I wasn't usually tongue-tied, but after saying that I was pleased and honored to accept her offer, about all I could do was grin like a Cheshire cat.

She smiled in return. "This brings me to what I hope is exciting news for you. What do you know about the Elm Hill Psychiatric Hospital for Women?"

"Just what I put in my paper, ma'am, since we live in another part of the state. It was founded as a small hospital during the Great Depression as a WPA project in what was considered a political coup for the mayor. I read the state news, since I come from here, so I saw the headlines last week. Certainly, the murder of Judge Adams and the immediate committal of his daughter to the hospital got my attention. Why wasn't she taken to the State Mental Hospital in Downsville? Since it's so much bigger and has many more violent patients, I would think that it should have more heavily secure wards."

"I can't read the mind of judges and policemen, but I would guess that it has to do with the character of the patient. Presumably, Carrie Adams' wealthy and influential family called in some favors to make sure that she escaped the electric chair and that their dirty laundry didn't get hung up in the Osloville Courthouse. Then again, I freely admit that I'm not an expert here. I study abnormal psychology, not abnormal politics."

She shook her head at her joke and then got back to business. "In any event, let's get away from last week's lurid events to the normal operations of Elm Hill as a successful mental institution. I became acquainted with their Director of Nursing, Carol Mason, in the late 1940s when she was a psychiatric nurse at Downsville. She wrote to me to ask for reading lists about abnormal psychology and mental hospitals. About six months after that, I invited her to a program that we sponsored on improving the treatment of mental health problems in our state. I was a little surprised when she said that she was coming. She seemed so eager and interested that I invited her to spend an extra day to attend a session of my Abnormal Psychology class.

"We then went out to dinner together. I thought we might compare our lives or gossip about certain prominent doctors. Instead, she treated me like a guru who could provide her insight and knowledge. She hadn't asked more than three questions before I became flabbergasted by how much she had read and absorbed and by how committed she was to improving the treatment of the mentally ill. She felt that too many of the patients in the huge state hospital were just being held in custodial care. She really yearned for better ways to help them. When I complimented her on how much she had learned and what she wanted to do, she cried. Evidently, since she was from a working class family, having a college professor praise her was seemingly overwhelming.

"We corresponded about every six months after that and met a couple of times. Three years ago, she moved to Elm Hill as a charge nurse in their Violent Ward. She was excited because she thought that the quality of care would be much better at a smaller semi-private hospital with more adequate staffing. I got the impression that she was both pleased about some things and disappointed about others. Then, after she was there just a year, she was promoted to Director of Nursing. She never explained how it happened, but, given her talent and determination, I thought that the Hospital Director made an inspired, if somewhat unorthodox, decision.

"Of course, after her promotion we began to talk about whether and how we could cooperate. Finally, last fall Miss Mason worked out an agreement that one of our doctoral students would work in their Violent Ward this summer as an informal nurses' aide. For somebody interested in abnormal psychology, this should be an invaluable opportunity. Early this semester I offered the position to a student who appeared interested. Then, three weeks ago, her boyfriend proposed and wanted a mid-summer wedding and honeymoon.

"I was at a loss for recruiting another doctoral student. Then I started reading your research project last Tuesday and jumped to the conclusion that, if you desired, you could pursue a very good career in abnormal psychology. I called Miss Mason on Thursday morning and asked if we could send someone who was just getting their B.S. and starting their graduate studies and if a young man could work as a nurses' aide. She said that she would have to consult with the Hospital Director and with several of the staff, but that she thought it could work. Then, she called back on Saturday to say that she had the Director's approval, but that you would probably have to put up with some hazing from the traditional Nurse Manager of the Violent Ward.

"Would you like to do it? It would give you invaluable experience and a jump start on our research project on psychiatric hospitals. They provide full room and board and the normal salary for a nurses' aide. That's not too much, but you'll have hardly any expenses."

"Thank you, Dr. Calder. It's an honor. I certainly am excited about an alternative to going home and working in the family drugstore for the summer. But what about the hazing? Should I be worried?"

She looked a little embarrassed. "Let me tell you about the nurses' aides at Elm Hill. Once Carol Mason became the Director of Nursing, she got the permission of the Hospital Director to begin hiring a few aides. These are young ladies with at least a high school education who might have an interest in a nursing career. If they work out as an aide, they can then be admitted to the Hospital's small Nursing School. From Miss Mason's and Elm Hill's perspective, while much of their work just substitutes for what the attendants do, they can quickly learn more advanced skills so they become much more valuable to the nurses. The drawback for you is that they have feminine uniforms with white pinafores over white blouses. Fortunately, the Nurse Manager of the Ward said you could wear a white shirt and white pants. However, like the nurses and nursing students, the aides are required to wear caps to keep their hair under control. Here, the Nurse Manager was less tolerant and decreed that you would need to wear a cap like the girls. It's a way of making you feel a little unwelcome. If anyone is mean to you, just tell Miss Mason. I get the impression that she's quite efficient in policing the staff."

I have to admit that I was a little taken aback about the idea of being capped, but that was far outweighed by the lure of working in a psychiatric hospital as a very valuable experience for starting an academic career in abnormal psychiatry. Also, the thought of treating the most notorious murderess in the state definitely had a lurid appeal.

"I think that it's a wonderful opportunity."

"I'm so glad you agree. You'll learn a great deal both about psychiatric disorders and their treatments and about organizational cultures that you most definitely can't get out of textbooks. I'm sure you'll have a wonderful summer.

"The committal of Carrie Adams to Elm Hill has changed things. Initially, the other student was supposed to work for three months from mid-June through mid-September between the end of our spring semester and beginning of our fall one. Now, Miss Mason wants someone right away to give more help to the ward. Luckily, you're a very diligent worker. You've finished your project and are doing extremely well in your two classes. Professor Metcalf agreed with me that both of us will give you A's in our classes if you take the Elm Hill internship and write short papers over the summer relating what you're doing at Elm Hill to our classes. How does that sound?"

"Ma'am you're overwhelming me with good news."

"When I said Elm Hill needs you right away, I wasn't understating the fact. They want you to take the bus up there tomorrow. There's one that leaves at 1:30 and gets there a little after four. So, you have tonight and tomorrow morning for packing. Once you get there, you'll have an orientation from Wednesday through Friday and then start work a week from today."

I was fairly efficient in packing and had everything but my toiletries ready by the time I went to bed. This gave me plenty of time Tuesday morning to go to the University Library and look at the back issues of the *Capital News* to get a much more detailed picture of the Adams murder. On the evening of the murder, Judge Daniel Adams and his wife Joyce attended a dinner in honor of Mayor Michael Meyers and gave a ride to their neighbor, the widow of Judge Thomas Ford. On their return, Marcia Ford accepted an invitation for a nightcap. However, as the three were walking along the driveway from the garage to the front door, Joyce stumbled and spilled her purse. Judge Adams went ahead, while the two women began to pick up the spilled items. They heard him open the front door and, almost immediately, the roar of a shotgun. Joyce and Marcia screamed and ran back along the driveway to an opening in the hedge between the Adams and Ford houses. They squeezed through and called the police from Marcia's home.

Two squad cars of police and an ambulance from Osloville Medical Center arrived within ten minutes of this call. The first officers on the scene found Judge Adams blown backwards onto the front porch by what turned out to be a double-barreled shotgun blast at very short range. They could see a figure sprawled in the entryway of the house. They approached and found that it was the Judge's daughter Carrie. She apparently had been flung backwards by the recoil of the shotgun, hit her head against the back of the entryway, and been knocked unconscious. She was covered with the blowback of her father's blood. The shotgun had been flung to the side of the entryway and had many of her fingerprints upon it. When the ambulance attendants came, they sedated her and carried her upstairs. Further investigation in the kitchen found evidence that she had used some unspecified drugs before committing the murder. She was then transported to the Elm Hill Psychiatric Hospital for Women by the order of Judge Melvin Welch. A few days later, an anonymous source in the Police Department claimed that Carrie's mother had confirmed that the Judge had been concerned by the girl's descent into drug abuse during her senior year in high school and had threatened to commit her to Elm Hill for treatment. This was followed over the next few days by wild speculations about the murder, as well as about drug parties and orgies among the students of Osloville High. However, there was little, if anything, concrete added to the basic facts that were initially reported.

Chapter 6 ~ Elm Hill

I normally would have enjoyed the bus ride to Osloville. The route went through farmland and two sets of rolling tree-covered hills that were green and beautiful in the late spring, even if the few small towns that we passed through were rather nondescript. Once I got on the bus in College City, however, my elation began to change to a significant amount of trepidation. I suddenly realized that I was entering a new world in which what I had done and learned in the past might not be of great value. I began to recall scenes from *The Snake Pit*, which I had seen several years earlier. What would I be expected to do? How should I act in an institution where dangerous patient outbursts or staff abuse might be around the corner in the next room or corridor? Certainly, I had almost no preparation for working in such an environment. These more somber thoughts kept me from enjoying the scenery and made me a little reluctant to descend from the bus in Osloville.

Dr. Calder had told me that I would be met by a tall Negro wearing white. At least it was easy to spot a man who was about six-two in a white shirt and white pants. More importantly from my perspective, he grinned and waved once our eyes locked and quickly moved to join me as I waited for my baggage to be unloaded at the side of the bus. We shook hands vigorously, but I noted that he didn't try to crush mine. His grin turned into a broad welcoming smile.

"Hi. You're Andy, right? Welcome to Osloville and Elm Hill. I'm, Clem Jones, the Chief Attendant. How much baggage do you have?"

"Hello, Mr. Jones. Thank you so much for meeting me. I've got two suitcases and a duffle bag. That's a little more than I can haul by myself comfortably."

"Well, that's not a worry. With four arms for three bags, we're in good shape."

Once we got to the car, Mr. Jones asked me what I knew about Osloville. When I admitted that I didn't know much, he provided a thumbnail sketch. "The town started about a hundred years ago. By the turn of the century, it was fairly prosperous as the agricultural and logging hub of the north central part of the state. The Great Depression did us in, like most places in the country. We've come back after the War. Farming's good and there's still some logging, but people are starting to realize that even though things are better, we're now a backwater to the industry in the southern part of the state. The downtown has come back from the Depression and, as you can see, is pretty nice. The city is now a little under 30,000, while it was almost 40,000 when the Depression hit.

"We're heading north now. That little rise a couple of miles to the right is Elm Hill. Then there's a longer ridge to the left. That's where the wealthy folks live. One of the reasons that the hospital was built on Elm Hill was that the rich folks who lived there before the Depression mostly went bust, so there was some nice property available."

"Thanks for being so friendly and informative."

He laughed infectiously. "You looked a little tense getting off the bus. I hope we aren't scaring you."

"This happened so fast. I only learned I was coming here yesterday. I was excited. Once I sat down on the bus, however, I started to wonder what I'd gotten myself into. Have you seen *The Snake Pit*?"

Mr. Jones laughed again, but not quite so heartily. "Yes, I've seen the movie and read the book, which is a little different. Well, they do a good job in showing that mental illness is real but that someone can get better from it. For example, almost all the long-term patients in the Violent Ward where you'll be working are substantially more troubled than Virginia was at her worst. In terms of our staff, I don't think we have any doctors who would get so involved in a single patient as the one in the movie, but, on the other hand, none of our staff are like the evil nurse. If she caught any of them being so abusive, Miss Mason would make sure that they, not the patient, got stuffed into a strait jacket. Really, our nurses generally care about the patients and are pretty nice to them unless they're strongly provoked. Some of the doctors are distant, but they certainly don't try to harm the patients. The only problem is some of the newer attendants who can get testy and nasty. It's not like before the War when they could hire good people as attendants."

I then asked him about his family. "Well, my wife works as a housekeeper up on Elm Hill. We're really pleased about our kids.

Michael graduated from high school two years ago and is now working as a linotype operator for the newspaper. That's a skilled occupation with decent pay. He's got a nice girlfriend who's a beautician. We're expecting them to get married before too long. Michelle will graduate from high school in a couple of weeks and is planning to go to Nursing School."

Once we reached the hospital, a guard waved at Mr. Jones as he opened the gate. We then entered, crossed the road that ran parallel to the hospital's front wall, and stopped about fifty feet after the crossing. We got out, grabbed the bags, and went through a gate into the back yard of a house that faced the road. The yard was far wider than I expected; it extended behind three structures. The first and the third were three-story wooden houses connected by a two-story brick building that jutted well into the back yard. Mr. Jones led me down steps going into the basement of the first house and then explained, "This whole conglomeration is Brackman Hall where the nurses, student nurses, and nurses' aides stay. Knocking down a nice house and putting that brick dormitory in the middle created a monstrosity if you ask me, but obviously nobody did. Since all the residents are women, we had a momentary problem with you. But Miss Mason insisted that you stay here rather than with the unmarried male attendants who aren't necessarily nice all the time. She had a storeroom here cleaned out to make a bedroom for you. Luckily, there's a bathroom down here as well. You've got a fairly large room that's sparsely furnished. The basement is locked off from the house above. Here's a key to the door we came in. As a word of warning, don't think that you can slip a nurse or other women in here. There's lots of snooping, peeking, and gossiping by the nurses."

On these not so cheery words of wisdom, we dropped my bags in the room that was spacious by university dormitory standards and exited the way we had come. Once we got back to the sidewalk, Mr. Jones got me oriented to the layout of the hospital grounds.

"The hospital was built during 1936-38 on four square blocks of homes that formed the top of Elm Hill. There aren't many of the old houses left, unfortunately, since I think that they're nice to look at. You can see the backs of the Brackman and Ryerson houses over the fence.

The Cobb house is further down and, like these two, it's attached to a brick dorm for the unmarried male and female attendants, as well as some staff members. The back half of this block is covered by gardens which the patients work. The block behind that has been turned into a park. As you can see, the trees around the houses were left. The block across from us has a variety of auxiliary buildings on it, four old houses plus some new buildings. I'm sure you'll find out a lot about them in the next few weeks. Finally, the hospital itself takes up most of the last square block. That's where we're going now. Why don't we stretch our legs a little? We can't park too much closer anyway."

I had seen several black-and-white photographs of Elm Hill Hospital while I was doing my senior research paper, but the reality was more impressive. The building filled almost an entire block and was made of bright red brick. Instead of a drab square structure, however, there were a variety of indents, rounded corners, and asymmetrical steeples that readily caught the eye that made it seem rambling and even a little winsome. It also reminded me of an old English mansion where Gothic horrors awaited innocent damsels. Similarly, I didn't see bars on the windows, so the hospital building didn't look particularly frightening, although I soon learned that the insides of all the windows on the wards were covered with strong mesh grills.

Mr. Jones quickly led me to a first-floor office suite. I followed him down a short corridor, around a corner, and into an office where a woman with dark curly hair who seemed about forty sat behind a nice wooden desk whose top was neatly kept. She rose and greeted Mr. Jones in a very familiar manner.

"Clem, it's great to see you. Thanks so much for getting Andy."

"He seems like a nice guy, Gwen. I think Miss Mason will like him. He's a little worried that he's not well enough prepared which, to my way of thinking, makes him sound pretty responsible and dedicated. Andy, this is Gwen Holdstrom, she's the secretary for the Director of Nursing. She's a good person. Let me leave you with her. I'm sure I'll see you around in the next few days."

"Thank you so much Mr. Jones. Let me return the compliment. You've made me feel a lot better about Elm Hill."

We shook hands and I turned to Mrs. Holdstrom, whose marital status was demonstrated by her wedding band and sparkling engagement ring. She, in return, gave me both a smile and a penetrating look from her brown eyes.

"Hello, Andy. We've heard such good things about you. Please don't worry. Miss Mason is smart enough so she won't get you involved in anything you're not ready for. Do you have anything you're worried about?"

"No, not really ma'am. Things just happened so fast, and this is entirely new to me. Thank you for being so welcoming."

"Well, I can certainly understand that. I've got a son eighteen and a daughter sixteen, so I know that young adults can face daunting new challenges in their lives. Maybe you can meet them later in the summer. I know they'd love to meet someone who's been at State U. Now, let's get to business. I hope you don't think that I'm rushing things, but I don't want to be late getting home. My husband worries about me. Like many people, he's a little scared about what goes on in a psychiatric hospital.

"Here are five pages of forms that you should fill out tonight and bring back tomorrow morning. We need these to get you into our employee system so you can get pay your and insurance. What about meeting here at nine tomorrow morning? I'll take you shopping and show you what you need to know about Osloville. Then you'll have lunch with Miss Mason, and she'll work with you in the early afternoon. Does that sound good?"

With that agreed, she smiled again, gave me a badge so I could go in and out the front door without being grabbed by the guard, asked me not to think of her as brusque, and showed me where the cafeteria was on the second floor.

Chapter 7 ~ My New Job

The next morning, wearing a blazer, white shirt, tie, and my almost best pants, I returned to her office. I received a nice welcome from Mrs. Holdstrom, especially when I produced a folder with the forms that I had filled out the previous evening. In return for the folder, she gave me an aides' cap and showed me how to wear it. She did make me feel better by telling me that I would only have to wear it on the ward.

We then went downtown for shopping. She showed me where the bus stops were and gave me a much more extensive tour than Mr. Jones had. Finally, we arrived at Thorne's Department Store to buy my uniform which, according to Mrs. Holdstrom, was provided by the hospital because its salaries, except for the doctors, were not overly generous. The shopping trip went well. I got shirts, pants, socks, shoes, and rainwear. Then, on the way back to Elm Hill, Mrs. Holdstrom pointed out that the white slip-on shoes were mandatory to prevent the patients from stealing shoelaces and then doing mischief with them. She also introduced me to another uniform regulation.

"Andy, you just use cotton underwear, don't you?"

"Yes, why do you ask?"

"Nurses, nursing students, and aides have to wear cotton panties and slips, but some girls like fancier nylon ones. The administration wants to make sure they don't wear them in order to prevent the patients from sneaking peeks and getting the wrong idea, but with just female patients that might not be a problem here. Before Miss Mason became Director of Nursing, the charge nurses would conduct lingerie checks a couple of times a year. I wouldn't be surprised if traditional Nurse Managers, like Miss Rayburn, may still do that more informally. Also, girdles are required for nurses, students, and aides who are putting on weight, but I don't think that you have a problem there."

When I got back to Miss Mason's office, she directed me to one of a pair of comfortable armchairs in a corner of her somewhat cluttered office. She was in her late 30s and was almost as tall as I am with wavy brown hair and a strong and determined face that, while not quite beautiful, was striking and attractive. She smiled in welcome, although in a somewhat business-like manner.

"Hello, Andy. Welcome to Elm Hill. I appreciate how quickly you got here. Dr. Calder thinks very highly of you. I think you'll work well here once you settle in, even if it seems strange at first. Today I want to tell you a little bit about Elm Hill and then go over what your duties will be. I'm sure you'll have some questions then. Since we only have until two, I think that that's all we can cover. Is that okay?"

"Yes ma'am. I'm glad to be here, but I feel a little lost."

She poured us a cup of coffee, which thankfully didn't need sugar. "Well, let's hope that you'll feel better once we chat. I'll start by giving you an overview of Elm Hill, which is helpful for understanding who the patients are and what their needs are. It was built as part of a WPA project which involved politics, as anything big usually does. Osloville had the contacts to get a good-sized WPA project, but didn't need schools or a federal building. The mayor got inspired by several scandals in Downsville in the early 1930s about the abuse of women patients. The result was a women's mental hospital whose operations would be only half financed by the state, with the other half of the budget covered by patient fees. This had several implications. The fact that there would be only female patients lessened the local opposition. I'm told that there were posters circulated of a crazed woman swinging an axe with the slogan, 'Keep Lizzie Borden down in Downsville.' The funding formula provided subsidized care for families who didn't want their loved ones confined in Downsville but simultaneously limited the patients to almost entirely upper and middle class women. Perhaps the most direct advantage is that we can have a significantly larger staff than the state facilities relative to our number of patients. I worked in Downsville before I came here, so I can honestly tell you that's there's no comparison in the quality of care that's given.

"Let me give you a sketch of how things work. The hospital is run by the doctors who prescribe the individual treatment for each patient and are supposed to meet with their patients at least once a week. The bulk of the care, of course, has to be provided by the nurses. While in theory we just carry out the orders of the doctors, in practice we have to exercise significant discretion. Doctors, for example, don't know or care much about how the wards are run.

"As a result, the nurses generally know much more about the patients than the doctors do. Still, we have to defer to them. For example, we *and* you have to stand up when a doctor comes into a room. At least you're lucky because they won't pat your bottom."

I wondered about her last statements which had been delivered in a neutral monotone. Sometime later, when I asked a nursing student about the doctors, she told me that the ones who liked to flirt limited themselves to girls who wanted their attention.

When I didn't respond, Miss Mason then concluded our morning discussion.

"Let me get Gwen to bring our lunches, and we can relax a bit." She then started asking questions about me that were both friendly and probing.

Once Mrs. Holdstrom picked up our trays at about 12:30, we got down to business about the Violent Ward and what I'd be doing there.

"There are ten wards. Each one has a Nurse Manager, who like me, works from nine to five unless there's an emergency. We have three eight-hour shifts: 7 a.m. to 3 p.m., 3 to 11, and 11 to 7. The wards have a charge nurse for each shift, plus some combination of nurses, nursing students, attendants, and nurses' aides.

"The Nurse Manager for the Violent Ward is June Rayburn. She doesn't get involved in the direct treatment of the patients unless there's an emergency. The one thing she does is to insert the tube for tube feedings because she feels, with some justification, that most of her charge nurses aren't adequately trained.

"I've added you to the day shift because that's where the most work is and because things got noticeably worse with Carrie Adams' admission. About three-quarters of the time that shift works Monday through Friday, but it has to change days periodically to coordinate with the two swing shifts that have some responsibility for the Violent Ward because, obviously, they can only work the weekend in a complex rotation. The charge nurse for your shift is Jane Greene, and Michelle Rice is a nurse who works under her. There are more nurses on most of the other wards, but we only have two on the Violent Ward because almost all the patients there are in custodial care and don't need intensive nursing. On the other hand, relatively few get shock therapy because that's used to help people get better, while most of the patients on the Violent Ward have little chance for improvement. In addition, Carly Henderson is a nursing student, Amy Strong is an aide, and Bertha Bartholomew and Thomas Reeves are attendants. Finally, while there are twenty-five cells or patient rooms in the Violent Ward; we've never had them all filled since I've been here. Right now, we have sixteen permanent residents, plus two more who have been sent there temporarily because seclusion didn't seem adequate for getting them under control. Do you have any questions so far?"

"No, except I don't know what a tube feeding is."

"When a patient can't or won't eat, they have to be fed by a tube that's put down into their stomach, but it's easy to get it into the lungs instead. That's why you need to have a well-trained doctor or nurse."

"Well, I'm glad that I'm not involved in that."

"Don't worry, Andy. You won't be assigned anything that's beyond your capability."

"That's a relief. What exactly will I do?"

"Miss Rayburn has detailed your responsibilities. She may not be particularly welcoming, but she's a responsible manager. Miss Rice and the other three women each have primary responsibility for specific patients. That's why they should be happy to see you because there will be one more person to share the work. As the new and inexperienced aide, you'll have three, but they will include the two problem patients, Mrs. Strickland and Miss Peters, who toss their food trays and even their bedpans at the people caring for them. Unfortunately for you, there's a tradition that the most junior aide or nursing student must run the risk in taking care of them. I would guess that you'll be presented with the surgeon's mask, rubber gloves, apron, and bathing cap that go with the job by Amy at seven sharp next Monday.

"The first thing that you have to do is wake them up at 7:30. Unless someone is in diapers or restraints, which none of your patients are at present, all you have to do is make sure that they're awake and put any dirty bedpans outside the door for Thomas to take away. Miss Rice and the other women then take the ones who aren't under watch to the bathroom area to clean up. In addition, on Tuesdays, Thursdays, and Saturdays, they get the patients showered as well.

"Once a week, on Monday, you also have to take and record their temperatures and blood pressures when they wake up. All our patients have their temperatures taken rectally to prevent someone from biting a thermometer. In the Violent Ward, moreover, they have to be restrained on their stomachs. I know this is a pain for both the patients and the staff, but we need to ensure their safety. Do you know how to read a thermometer?"

"Yes ma'am, but I've never taken anyone's temperature like that. Also, I don't know how to take blood pressure."

"Don't worry. They'll show you how. That part's easy at least. Also, you're responsible for keeping the 'census' for your three patients. Each day you'll be given cards for each of them by Mrs. Greene that has entries for each half hour. You have to record where they are at that time. For example, you'll start at seven when all three should be in their rooms unless something bizarre is happening. Then you have to visually check each half hour after that.

"Once the patients are ready for the day, which obviously varies in time quite a bit, breakfast is served. Take trays to Mrs. Strickland and Miss Peters who have to eat in their rooms because they can become quite disruptive. Then go back to the breakfast room to have your own breakfast with Mrs. Smith, unless she's out of control and confined to her room. After breakfast most of the patients go to the lounge or the dayroom for the morning, while a few are confined to their cells or just stay in them voluntarily. Mrs. Strickland and Miss Peters have the choice of staying in their rooms or being restrained in iron anklets in the day room. If they want to go to the day room, you have to escort them and put on their anklets. If they don't, they join what's called the 'parade' where the patients who are staying in their rooms are walked around the ward for twenty minutes.

"Hydrotherapy starts between 9:00 and 10:00 depending on the day. Because it seems to calm our most troubled patients, the doctors are quite liberal in ordering it for patients on the Violent Ward. Generally, all six tubs are full for two-hour sessions in the morning. The women set up the tubs and get the patients into and out of them. You need to help monitor patients in the tubs in an informal rotation that is interspaced with your other work, such as monitoring the lounge and dayroom and keeping your census. You may also have to help in packing a patient or wrapping them in cold wet sheets to help calm them down. I'd suggest wearing rubber gloves if you're sensitive to the cold.

"Lunch is at 12:15 and is just like breakfast. When it's over, about 1:00, all the patients have to go back into their rooms until the end of the shift at 3:00. Some read or nap. Indeed, most receive light sedation. You'll use that time to write up your nurse's notes on your three patients. You'll get fairly detailed sheets to fill in from Miss Rayburn. This brings us to the last task that you might have to perform. Miss Rayburn is a strong believer in enemas. You'll find that you and the people taking care of them on other shifts have to record bowel movements. Administering an enema is not that hard, so I'm sure that they can show you how to do it.

"Even though none of your patients are in diapers at present, you'll probably have to apply and change a few. I'm a strong believer in diapers for incontinent patients. When I was at Downsville, the messes that our incontinent people made, sometimes on purpose, were horrible. Diapers are much better for the patients and much less work for the staff than cleaning up all the time. Thus, I've made them mandatory for those who display problems. By the way, this brings us to something that you won't normally have to do. This is changing bed linens, which is an extra chore in the Violent Ward because you have to take off and put back on the two straps around the bed for the wrist and ankle cuffs. Unless there's a huge mess in the bed that needs immediate attention, that's the responsibility of the evening shift.

"I've tossed a lot at you. For Thursday and Friday morning, you'll go to the Violent Ward and observe what they do. Carly Henderson will give you training on your major tasks and will give you a chance to practice. Is there anything that you don't think that you can handle?"

"It sounds like I should have a chance to get into the swing of things over the next couple of days. Is Carly cooperative?"

"I think she'll be helpful. She has a sweet disposition and seems concerned about her patients.

"Now comes what I hope you'll think of as good news. Miss Rayburn has agreed that you only have to work on the ward through lunch. Once the patients are back in their rooms, all you really have to do is paperwork. Thus, when you finish your notes and give them to Mrs. Greene, you should come up to Gwen's office and help us as my assistant.

"Finally, I've got some homework for you, which shouldn't be as burdensome as it would be for the normal incoming aide or nursing student. These two booklets are the *Ward Manual* and *Ward Routine,* which Mrs. Rayburn has developed. They're far more extensive than the ones for most of the other wards. I don't think that they're intended to be read in a sitting. Instead, skim the general topics and then use them as a reference book. The book is a text on psychiatric nursing by Katharine Steele. I can't put enough emphasis on her central theme that we must be caring, respectful, and sympathetic toward our patients at all times."

Before I left, I asked her if we could work out some arrangement so that I could attend my graduation on the second Saturday in June and my sister Jennifer's high school graduation the following Monday evening. Much to my relief, she said that there shouldn't be any problem and that I could work extra hours later to make up for the time I missed.

Chapter 8 ~ Into the Swing of Things

After supper I returned to my room for my reading assignments, which had the comfort of familiarity with my academic life. The booklets struck me as comprehensive and a major work of love by Miss Rayburn. What was really striking, and more than a little daunting, was the daily Behavioral Chart of sixty items which we had to fill in. Clearly the patients were under very close supervision. In addition, I was also surprised, even after a course on abnormal psych, to learn from the nursing text that half the hospital beds in America are in psychiatric hospitals and wards.

My orientation and first week actually went quite smoothly. I walked to the hospital on Thursday with Carly, a petite and pretty woman a year out of high school. She clearly was quite competent, and showed me how to find the breakfast and lunch trays, take blood pressure and rectal thermometer readings, administer enemas, monitor hydrotherapy, apply and change diapers, and use bed restraints, restraining belts, and the iron anklets that were attached to two benches in the day room. In addition, she introduced me to many of the patients, but not to several "dangerous" ones including the two that were notorious: Carrie Adams and Jenny Sachs. They stood out in their prison-striped hospital gowns, designating that they had been committed as criminally insane, and restraints, a strait jacket for Carrie and a heavy leather restraining belt for Jenny. She also warned me about "Mean Monica," a more than occasionally violent paranoid schizophrenic who had won infamy for tossing a food cart in one of her rages. She certainly was no stranger to packs and strait jackets.

On our way into work on Friday, I asked her what she thought about *Psychiatric Nursing*. She agreed strongly with Miss Mason that the book brought home the importance of treating our patients with respect and kindness. Indeed, she had really been moved by how the nurses in a case study changed their treatment of patients after reading a book, Jane Hillyer's *Reluctantly Told*. On the other hand, she wondered how anyone who had worked in a mental hospital could downplay the need for restraints the way Mrs. Steele did.

"We have to use leather straps for restraints to keep agitated patients from chewing through them. I know that when I was in Nursing School, we were told that packing was a treatment rather than a restraint, but in reality it totally immobilizes a patient. Even strait jackets are necessary for violent patients like Mean Monica and that murderess Carrie Adams. I like the old saying that a strait jacket is just a snuggle with straps." She was so deadpan that I couldn't tell whether or not the last sentence was an example of nursing humor. I asked her how the patients responded to restraints.

"Over half don't like them but accept restraint as part of their treatments. Maybe a third get more agitated and out-of-control when they're restrained. Actually, they hate packs worse than strait jackets. There're also a few who calm down when they're restrained. Surprisingly, that Mean Monica is one of them."

The next week I started my duties for real and quickly got into the rhythm of the ward. Miss Rayburn had certainly been insightful enough to give me work that I could do while assigning me enough duties that both my co-workers and I felt that I was contributing.

While the world of a psychiatric ward is certainly strange, the way in which Miss Mason and Miss Rayburn integrated me into working life at Elm Hill made the transition much smoother than it might have been. Carly prepared me well by passing on such light-hearted but insightful adages as: "Don't think it strange if you see patients talking or shouting to themselves." Or, "When dealing with patients, disbelieve 90% of what you hear and 75% of what you see." She also told me about a former nurse under Miss Rayburn, now a patient in the dementia ward, who now spent her days asking other patients about their bowel movements. Consequently, when a slightly agitated patient addressed me in an incoherent "word soup" on my first day, I just smiled, patted her gently on her arm and shoulder, and was rewarded with a smile in return. Carly had a patient who, in her calmer moments, would come up to her, pat her on the forearm, and whisper, "One, two, three, four, five." Carly would then whisper back, "Six, seven, eight, nine, ten." Then, the patient would walk away giggling.

I also started forming positive relationships with several of my patients. Mrs. Strickland seemed so glad that I was much gentler and more caring than Amy that, from what I had heard, she calmed down appreciably. Mrs. Smith was depressed and not initially communicative, but by the end of my first week I was getting her to laugh about stories, more fictional than real, of wild sorority girls at State U. She hadn't gone to college and, as a religious woman, enjoyed feeling that maybe she was the better for it. In contrast, Miss Peters, a paranoid schizophrenic, was hard to reach and made me glad that I was wearing a bathing cap on Thursday.

The staff on our shift was something of a mixed bag as workmates. Carly was quite helpful and became friendlier as the days passed. Big Bertha was about sixty and had steel gray hair. She was as tall as I was and perhaps a little humiliatingly, more muscular. She was polite but not too friendly. Carly said that she was nice to her and speculated that she might by awed by all my education. In contrast, Thomas and Amy, a tall blonde, were openly unfriendly, if not hostile. Thomas didn't want to have anything to do with me. Amy, for her part, shot demeaning comments in my direction on a regular basis, as she did, to a lesser extent, to Carly and Bertha. She also gave me a nasty sneer as we passed in a corridor after I had been in the ward a few days and warned that I shouldn't try to chase that hussy Carly because everyone knew that she was having a secret affair, perhaps with a doctor. The Nurse Manager and the two shift nurses were polite but not particularly friendly. As Carly told me, this was to be expected because the "black bands," so named for the black stripes on the caps of RNs, considered themselves far superior to students, attendants, and aides. Actually, the neutral treatment that I got from Miss Rayburn was a pleasant surprise. I also learned several more examples of how the doctors enjoyed an exalted status at Elm Hill, as Miss Mason had indicated during my first interview with her.

My first week went surprisingly smooth and I settled into the routine that existed in even the Violent Ward. I mastered my assigned tasks without much difficulty and quickly learned that I had enough to do so that I didn't wonder or worry very much about what others were doing. At the strong suggestion of both Miss Rayburn and Mrs. Greene, I backed away when a patient became overly agitated and aggressive and called for an attendant, but this only happened twice during my first week. I noticed that Bertha could both restrain and calm a violent patient, but that Thomas, despite his ability to get a patient into physical restraints, seemed to provoke more resistance from his charges. Patient outbursts were almost always followed by packing or wrapping them completely and tightly in wet sheets by either Mrs. Greene or Miss Rice. At least during my first week, I didn't participate in or directly witness any packings, but the other staff members felt that they were much more effective and humane than a restraining belt or a strait jacket in calming agitated patients.

I also got the impression, although nobody told me, that the staff used strict routines to keep the patients as calm and controlled as possible. Uncertainty evidently upset the patients and led to conflict and outbursts. Even in my first few days at Elm Hill, I observed how one agitated woman could spread chaos through the ward. I did note that even the patients who didn't need restraints had little to do with one another. Without social support from other patients, therefore, the inmates of the Violent Ward were more at risk of being set off than the residents of other wards who had developed social ties and support among themselves.

My work for Miss Mason during my first week was much less challenging and stressful. In fact, she told me that I would be given harder assignments later but that she wanted me to settle in first. I worked for her from about one to three in the afternoon when my shift ended. Sometimes, she would simply describe what she was doing or have me sit in on a meeting to give me a better feel for how Elm Hill operated. I also helped Mrs. Holdstrom with some of her duties. In particular, she had me run errands to various parts of the hospital so I would get to understand it better, encouraging me to take my time coming back and to chat with people informally if I had the chance. I think, but was afraid to ask, that she and Miss Mason felt that this would both help me understand Elm Hill's culture and make me less alien to the hospital's staff. Certainly, I had several enjoyable short chats with nurses, attendants, secretaries, and even a doctor, as well as finding out where drinkable coffee was available.

At the end of my second week on the job, I got an indirect indication that I was accepted. Carly noted that I had to be in my bathing cap for the first part of the morning and asked me to pose with the four women who had to wear swim suits and caps when they showered the patients. Evidently, Carly, Bertha, and Amy physically washed each patient, while Miss Rice supervised those who waited in the adjoining large bathroom facilities. On the next day, I waited until all the patients had been showered and taken back to their rooms and then posed in the showers with them, making sure that I kept Big Bertha between Amy and myself. The picture was posted on one of the bulletin boards. Mrs. Greene complimented me for being such a good sport, and I even got pleasant teasing from several patients.

Chapter 9 ~ A Council of War

On the Thursday of my first full week, Miss Mason invited me to dinner at the Holdstroms. On Sunday afternoon she picked me up in front of Brackman Hall, along with a shy nurse named Emma Hughes. The Holdstroms lived in an impressive two-story brick house. Mrs. Holdstrom's husband Peter was about ten years older than she was with dark graying hair and the beginning of a paunch. He was Vice President of Osloville Bank. Despite his high position, he seemed friendly and down-to-earth. He joked that his bank attracted all of the Norwegians, half the Germans, but none of the Swedes in the county. Their two children were slim and average height and had dark hair like their parents. Peter Jr. was a senior at Osloville high, and Helen was a sophomore. They sat on either side of me at dinner and peppered me with questions about State U. since Peter was going there in September as a math major. The party was completed about ten minutes after our arrival when Mr. Jones arrived in his pick-up truck.

After dinner, Mrs. Holdstrom said that it was time for business and led us to the back of the house to a large library room with just enough comfortable chairs to seat us all. A coffee service set on a table and almost everyone availed themselves. Miss Mason began the meeting in a business-like tone.

"Thanks for coming. All of us, except Andy, were involved in bringing Carrie Adams to Elm Hill after her father's murder. Clem even gave us the name of 'Black Angels' because the huge storm that night had us wearing black rubber wardrobes and because we brought her to a place of refuge, even if it's not heaven where the real angels are. I think that that's symbolic and unfortunately true.

"Most of you have some idea how strange her committal was. She was whisked away from the police by order of a conservative and pro-police judge. In fact, the investigating officers weren't even notified until she was safely confined in our Violent Ward. Clem and I took her away from police custody and transported her here, which is almost certainly unprecedented in Elm Hill's history."

A few people nodded while Miss Mason took several sips of coffee before she continued. "The investigation of the murder is strange as well. The police believe that Carrie murdered her father, presumably because he was cracking down on her escalating drug use. Yet, as all of you except Andy know, there are certainly some important facts that seem fairly incongruent with this theory. That's why I brought us together today away from any prying eyes or ears so that we can talk things over. Clem, why don't you go first?"

"I've looked into several things over the last couple of weeks. First, at Carol's suggestion, I asked the four Negro officers to let us know anything significant about the investigation. We hit pay dirt with your suggestion that there was something funny about Carrie's dress. Jimmy Clay, one of the policemen who were assigned to search the property the next morning, was on the lookout for something that might explain it. What he found buried in an outside garbage can was a woman's clear plastic raincoat that had light stains on it most of the way up, but heavier stains around the top and the collar. He's pretty quick minded and concluded that it was worn under the dress, which would seem crazy unless the murderer wanted to plant the dress on an innocent victim. He told Detective Perkins about it when nobody was around. Perkins then got the raincoat into an evidence bag without making a fuss about it. Now it's sitting in the evidence room, but nobody except Jimmy has any idea that it's significant.

"Second, the police are totally convinced that Carrie is the murderess. They're enraged that she was committed to Elm Hill, but nobody is going to challenge Judge Welch. I haven't been able to talk directly to anyone who was in the house right after the murder, but the gossip, which hasn't been contradicted by those investigators, is that there were traces of powder cocaine in the kitchen. Thus, the conclusion is that Carrie snorted cocaine before killing her father, which might explain why a light sedative knocked her out if it interacted badly with the cocaine. Mrs. Adams, moreover, has confirmed in a written deposition that the Judge caught Carrie using drugs, though she doesn't know the specifics, and that both of them were increasingly concerned about her wild behavior over the last few months."

"Well, Clem. That's good news. It's always nice when one of your suppositions turns out to be true. Also, it's good to hear about the cocaine allegation because it raises another indication that there's something suspicious about the police theory. The morning after we brought Carrie to the hospital I had the Admission nurses take blood and urine samples and take detailed pictures of her body while they were processing her. We don't have an adequate lab to test the blood, but I have a good friend at the Medical Center who was happy to help. There was no evidence of recreational drugs, including cocaine. However, she had been given a strong dose of the sedative sodium amytal which explains why she was knocked out for so long. In addition, the pictures clearly show that she was given two injections in her right arm. My friend at the Medical Center confirmed that their ambulance attendants only gave her one light sedative, so somebody else must have injected the sodium amytal. Yes, Gwen?"

"This isn't definitive, but I asked Peter about Carrie because she's in three of his classes this semester. He said that she's a super student and that he didn't see any signs of drug use or degeneration. Just a few days before the murder, for example, her essay on *Bleak House* was praised by Mrs. Grossman as the best in the class. It's hard, if not impossible, to believe that she could have done such work if the police claims are true."

Miss Mason then continued, "Well, Clem, we interrupted you. Do you have anything else?"

"Yes, there are two more things. My wife Ella works as a housekeeper at the other end of River Ridge and she hears a lot of gossip from both the servants and the owners. A couple of the other rich kids who live up there are definitely wild, but nobody had ever even whispered anything like that about Carrie before the murder. There has been gossip over the last couple of years that the Adams' marriage was not ideal. He was much more well-liked than she. At first, she was rumored to be spending his money but not giving him all her love. Then more recently, somebody claimed that he had been seen kissing their cute maid, Patty, in their backyard.

"Second, I've obviously been keeping my eyes open about the hospital. Carrie's committal stirred up a lot of emotion and gossip, which is to be expected, but I get the feeling that there's more happening as well. For example, there was even more of an uproar than would have been expected when a social worker plopped herself down at the doctors' table three weeks ago. People started all sorts of wild rumors about what she was up to. Likewise, some of the attendants feel that there are big changes coming, although they're not sure what they are. Thomas and Carl in the Violent Ward have been openly insolent to poor Carole Blaine, the Assistant Director of Attendants, who's certainly a good-hearted soul. Thomas told her that he wouldn't have to take her guff much longer."

Emma interjected, "He's horrible. Two days after I went with Miss Mason to visit Carrie on her first morning here he was waiting for me when I came off my night shift. He accosted me when I left the ward and told me that he'd take care of me if I tried to interfere in his ward again. Then he looked at me like I was a prostitute and said that he knew what to do with girls like me. Please ma'am. He's a creep. He frightens me. Is he doing what Miss Rayburn wants?"

Miss Mason got up with a grim look on her face, walked over to Emma's chair, and laid her arm protectively around the nurse's shoulder. "Emma, I'm so sorry that you had to suffer this. However, Dr. Rydberg has already talked to Miss Rayburn about Thomas. If she ever had any use for him, she doesn't anymore. If Thomas threatens you again, just tell me. I don't think he will. Miss Rayburn can be pretty direct in telling people that they better stay out of trouble. Is there anything else, Emma?"

"Well, ma'am. I took your advice to stay away from the Violent Ward and not ask anything about Carrie. Still, Michelle Rice has been cold to me since then. She seems to think that I'm part of some conspiracy against Miss Rayburn."

"That's interesting, Emma. But I can't make much sense out of it. Does someone have a guilty conscience? If so, is it about Carrie's treatment, the ward itself, or about political games in the hospital? There may or may not be something going on, but what it could be is utterly beyond me right now."

Miss Mason then lightened the mood.

"Andy, you're a Black Angel now, aren't you? Didn't you wear your slicker and boots on Monday?" A couple of people smiled and Mrs. Holdstrom said that she would have Debbie bring in cookies and more coffee to sweeten the atmosphere. I have to admit that even after a large dinner the thought of refreshment and breaking the tension seemed very attractive. We spent a little more time in small talk. Finally, when good spirits had been recovered, Miss Mason said that we might be interested in Carrie's police interview and switched on a tape player. The tape began with a woman's voice.

"Here's Carrie Adams, detectives. Carrie, that's Detective Perkins on your right and Detective Kempton on your left. They need to ask you about the night of your father's murder. Miss Weiss, could you please remove Carrie's gag. I'll meet you at the nurses' station when we're done."

After a short pause for the nurse to leave the room, Detective Perkins took over the questioning. "Do you know why we're here?"

"Yes, sir. You're investigating my father's murder. A nurse told me about it early this morning."

"We need to know what happened last night. What's your story?"

"Dad and Mom went out at about seven. The staff had a night out so I was alone. I studied my calculus and chemistry in my room. I'm good at literature and history, but I need to study math and science pretty hard. I was planning to watch a TV show at nine, so about 8:45 I went downstairs. I was going into the kitchen to get a snack before my show started. I remember opening the kitchen door, but the next thing I remember was waking up in a padded room here, wearing a strait jacket and strapped to the bed."

"What were you going to have for your snack?"

"Cookies and eggnog."

"Do you remember whether you had it?"

"No, sir."

"Would you have washed up your plate and glass?"

"Not normally, but with Mrs. Larson and Patty out, I would have."

"There were an apron and rubber gloves by the sink. Would you have used them?"

"Yes, sir. I put them on automatically."

"Would you have put the dish and glass away?"

"No, I would have washed and dried them, but left them in the drying rack."

"There was nothing in the drying rack and the dishpan was bone dry when we got there. How can you explain that?"

"I can't sir. I don't remember anything after I opened the kitchen door."

"When was the last time you washed up in the evening?"

"It would be over a month ago. Usually, one or both of our women servants are there."

"What do you remember about coming to Elm Hill, Carrie?"

"I don't remember anything until I woke up. I had a major headache. A little later a young nurse came in. She was dressed in protective clothing. I don't know why. She looked mean but didn't say anything. She sat me up and attached my jacket to the wall with a short chain. Then she opened my mouth and got the gag in place and, finally, put leg straps on me. I was so frightened. Almost immediately, two other nurses came in. The older one asked me a couple of questions. I could only nod yes or no because of the gag."

"What did she ask?"

"She asked if I knew I was Carrie Adams, and I nodded yes. She asked if I knew that I was in Elm Hill Psychiatric Hospital for Women, and I didn't know what to respond. Finally, she asked if I knew whether my Daddy had been murdered, and I started to cry. She seemed kind. She patted me a little and made sure that the jacket and gag weren't hurting me."

"What else happened today?"

"A little later the young nurse took me to Admissions. After that, she brought me back to my room and took off the restraints. She told me that the doctor had said that I don't need to be restrained in my cell during the day, but I better be careful and not cause any trouble because she had the authority to truss me up again."

"Do you remember before last night, Carrie?"

"Yes, sir. At least I think I do."

"Okay, now tell me about the fights you had with your father about your escalating drug use. First, he caught you with marijuana and then he found out that you had started snorting cocaine."

"That's not true." We could easily hear the rising combination of fear and anger in her voice. "I've never used drugs. Daddy never believed it. Mom and Daddy had a big fight in March. Mrs. Larson and I heard them screaming. Toward the end, she accused him of letting me run wild and become a criminal. She said that Patty had led me astray to get back at her. A few days later Daddy called me into the law library he keeps at home. I told him that I wasn't having sex with Johnny, that I was afraid to touch any illegal drugs, and that I was still getting very good grades in school. He kissed me, told me that he believed me, and said that Mom loved me but was upset about other things. I don't have fights with my parents. Really, I don't."

"There was powder cocaine on the kitchen counter. That indicates you were snorting it."

"No, no! I told you I don't do drugs."

"It must have been done after the dinner dishes were washed up or it would have been cleaned away. Who else could have done it? Was your Mom right? Is Patty a drug addict?"

"No, sir. Please believe me. She's like me. She doesn't even smoke."

"Why do you think you're here and tied up like a wild animal?"

"You must think that I killed Daddy, but I didn't. I love him."

"How was he murdered?"

"I don't know. The older nurse just said that he was killed."

"Your amnesia is very convenient, missy, but you're out of our reach here. Laura, can you get her back to her cell?"

There was a momentary silence as the two women presumably left the room. Then Detective Kempton spoke for the first time since the interview started. "You shouldn't have let her off so easy. That rich bitch is making us look like fools."

"Take it easy, Matt. We're all frustrated that a killer of a wonderful man is escaping justice, but isn't it clear to you that the people who run this city want it this way? Somebody in the Police Department must be cooperating with them. Unfortunately, they're the ones who make and bend the rules and pay our salaries into the bargain. What we need to do is make sure we have an airtight case, so if she ever steps out of her whacko ward, she'll be whisked to the electric chair before she knows what's happening. We're almost there. I'm pretty sure we caught her in a major lie. I'm almost certain that some of the high school rowdies will tattle on her drug use."

Miss Mason shut off the tape machine and turned to me. "Well, Andy. Can you describe how Carrie is treated?"

"Carrie spends most of her time in her cell. As far as I can tell, Amy Strong, the nurses' aide, is the one in charge of her. She's the one who gets her up and takes her meals to her. She's also the one who escorts her when she's out of her room. For example, she puts her into a strait jacket and gag and walks her around for twenty minutes after breakfast. I'm pretty sure that last week this walk or 'parade' was the only time Carrie was not confined to her cell during our shift. Incidentally, Amy stopped gagging her on Wednesday. I haven't seen Miss Rayburn or Mrs. Green show any special interest in her. Also, I'm not even sure who her doctor is. I'm so busy with my own work that I can't be sure from my own observation, but I think that there would be gossip if nurses or doctors were going in and out of her room during the day.

"According to Carly Henderson, most of the other patients and even some of the staff are afraid of her. That's why they're happy that Amy has been given charge of her. She's nasty, as I've found out, but many patients seem to feel that she can keep the murderess under control. The patients and staff feel that Carrie's so violent that treatment probably won't do any good. Consequently, they think she'll be warehoused here for the rest of her life, so the hospital's main objective should be protecting other patients and the staff from her."

"The poor girl. One unfortunate thing, though, is that we can't even hint that she may not be guilty. As to who's her doctor, Dr. Carson admitted her and is still in charge of her treatment, as far as I know. He probably hasn't consulted much with her, though. He doesn't give that much individual attention to his patients after the initial diagnosis. In addition, I'm sure he knows that Dr. Rydberg will be doing Carrie's psychiatric evaluation. Since someone will have to give very unpopular testimony in court, Dr. Rydberg wouldn't put anyone else in that position. Realistically, his position in the community means that nobody would think about retaliating against him. In general, by the way, doctors spend less time with their patients on the Violent Ward than they do with others who have a much better prognosis. Thus, it may be a little difficult to figure out which doctor is treating which patient if you're not Miss Rayburn or Mrs. Greene."

"Oh, there's one other thing about Carrie. She's starting a series of electro-shocks next week. Since not many of our patients get shock treatments, there's been gossip about it. Why would they do that? I've read that electro-shock can interfere with short-term memory, which makes us wonder about administering it to someone suffering from amnesia."

Emma said, "I think that's true from my experience. A lot of the patients on Ward 6 get electro-shock. It helps many improve enough to go home, but loss of memory is one of the things that they complain about."

Again, by mutual consent, we sat back as Emma walked around pouring coffee, while several people helped themselves from the plate of cookies. When everyone was settled, Gwen cleared her throat.

"Everyone's contributed to our puzzle except me. Miss Mason asked me to check out any politics or problems at Elm Hill that might be connected to the murder or Carrie's confinement. You can't work at Elm Hill for long without finding out there's always a buzz and political intriguing, but the political games are almost always just noise and don't lead to anything. I'm good friends with Denise Nuxhall, Dr. Rydberg's head secretary. I asked her casually about the Board. Judge Adams didn't seem to be involved in any squabbles, but there is a troublesome issue on the horizon. Bernard Ernst, the big guy in real estate, is starting to make noises that the doctors who practice here but aren't on our permanent staff should have more control over the hospital's administration. He claims that they represent and understand the community far better than the doctors on permanent staff. Ernst is a close friend with Dr. Carmichael who has six patients here and an obnoxious personality. Thus, Ernst is probably pushing his friend's agenda. Judge Adams would have supported Dr. Rydberg completely against this interference, but so would almost all the other Board members. Dr. Carmichael does have a patient on the Violent Ward and did demand that Carly be fired or disciplined for putting her into a restraining belt, but that was long before the murder.

"Dr. Rydberg has become increasingly concerned by all this commotion and wonders if there might be something wrong in the hospital. Thus, he's asked several people to go over things. In particular for me, since the hospital uses Osloville Bank, he's having Peter get the bank to audit our accounts. So far, all the money that should have gone into the account has, but there may be some problems with a couple of transfers out. We should know within a week or so, but again there doesn't seem to be any direct connection to Judge Adams."

Chapter 10 ~ Interrogation

Monday began in a tumultuous fashion as we had three manic outbursts before lunch. Fortunately for me, none of my patients were involved. Both Bertha's muscles and her soft tones were put to good use, and I would guess that Mrs. Greene's arms got a little sore from all her wrapping. About 11:00, just after hydrotherapy had ended and we thought that the ward was calming down, Big Bertha came up to me and said that she and I were supposed to get Carrie ready for her first electro-shock session because Amy had been called to Admissions to help with a hallucinating and violent patient. We detoured to the main entrance to the ward where someone had left a rolling stretcher to convey Carrie to her shock treatment. We pushed it to her room and went in. She was sitting on her chair and looked tense and, once she saw us, a little surprised. I spoke to her kindly, trying to make her feel a little better.

"Hello, Carrie. I'm Andy Russell, a nurses' aide, and this is Bertha Bartholomew. We're going to get you ready for your treatment. Miss Strong had to go somewhere else so she can't take you like she usually does. Is that okay?"

"Yes, sir. I'm ready." She got up and held out her arms, evidently expecting to be straitjacketed.

"No, Carrie. You don't need that this time because you'll be restrained to a rolling stretcher."

Bertha took her out the door and helped her up on the stretcher. Once she was strapped down, I squeezed her hand, hoping to reassure her. She squeezed back and smiled at me. Following Bertha's instructions, I wheeled the girl down the hall to the front of the basement where I turned left and headed toward a nurse with thick glasses and bangs who seemed to be waiting for us. She was in her thirties and seemed quite businesslike.

"Hello, I'm Mrs. Garson. You must be Andy Russell. I've heard a lot about you. I was expecting Miss Strong, though. I understand that she's the one in charge of the patient. Have you ever brought a patient in for electro-shock before?"

"No, ma'am. I haven't."

"Well, just bring her into the waiting room. Then when she's ready in the recovery room, we'll call you too pick her up."

I was tempted to squeeze Carrie's hand again but decided that I probably shouldn't do it in front of the no-nonsense Mrs. Garson. Before I could push the stretcher again, however, there were soft footsteps behind me. Miss Mason's voice floated over my shoulder.

"Hello, Helen. Have you got everything under control as usual?"

"Yes, ma'am. We're right on schedule. Doctor Carson is really good at this. We're starting shock treatments for Carrie Adams right now."

"I'm sorry to disrupt your schedule, but here's a written order from Dr. Rydberg canceling the shock treatments for Miss Adams. He felt that it might well be counterproductive to impose electro-shock on someone with what we hope is temporary amnesia. The police may want to question her any day. Do you understand?"

"Yes, ma'am, of course. Excuse my asking, but why did you bring this down here yourself?"

"Well, to be candid, I was afraid that you might not accept an order from Gwen. Then we'd have a real problem. Wouldn't we?"

"Please, ma'am. I don't want to get involved in politics. I do what Dr. Carson tells me because that's what I'm supposed to do."

"I know you're a very good nurse, Helen."

Mrs. Garson turned, walked a short way down the hall and went into the electro-shock suite. Miss Mason then leaned over Carrie and said softly.

"Hello, Carrie? Do you remember me?"

"Oh, yes ma'am. You were so nice."

"I still think that you may be in danger, so don't trust anyone in the Violent Ward except Andy. How does Amy Strong treat you?"

"She's horrible. I'm scared of her, but I'm pretty sure that she doesn't doubt my amnesia."

"We can't talk much longer, but do you remember anything more than you told the police?"

"Not much, but I'll tell you if it helps. I do remember going into the kitchen and having three cookies and a glass of eggnog. I did wash up afterwards and put on the apron and rubber gloves. Then I dumped out the dishpan, took off the gloves, and dried the glass and plate. Suddenly, I felt extremely tired. The last thing I remember is turning toward the table in the kitchen so I could sit down. Is that helpful?"

"I think so, Carrie. I'd guess that someone drugged your eggnog. I'll check with the police to see what happened to the bottle. Goodbye and good luck."

As I wheeled her back to the ward, I squeezed her hand again. She looked up, smiled, and then brought a blank expression back to her face as we entered the ward where people could see her.

Given the unexpectedly hectic morning, I was ready to relax when I got to Mrs. Holdstrom's office at 1:45. However, she was looking serious and told me that the police were coming to interview Emma Hughes at 3:30, which had Miss Mason worried because she couldn't think of any reason for interrogating her. She had me run several and probably pointless errands. Then at about 3:15 Miss Mason led both of us to a door that was labeled "Janitor's Closet" at the back of the administrative suite. After checking that nobody else was in view and telling us to keep absolutely quiet, she unlocked and opened the door and let us into a small room with four swivel chairs around a table. After about ten minutes, she must have received a signal of some kind that I missed because she rose and clicked a switch on the back wall which evidently activated a tape recorder in the next room. We heard a door opening followed by what I now recognized as Detective Perkins' voice.

"Thank you, Denise. Could you please bring her in now?"

"Certainly, sir. Would you like refreshments?"

"Just some water would be fine."

After a pause of a minute or two, Emma evidently came into the room. "Hello, Miss Hughes. I'm Detective Perkins. With me are Detective Kempton and Policewoman Sanders. Officer, would you please seat her and stay next to her."

"Yes, sir."

We heard some chairs scrape before Detective Perkins started the interrogation.

"Miss Hughes, we're investigating the murder of Judge Adams and think that you have information that might be valuable to us. Are you willing to cooperate?"

"Of course, sir."

"Detective Kempton will do the questioning."

"I understand that you already have had a bad experience with the police. If you tell the truth now, you won't get in any more trouble, but if you lie you'll be back in handcuffs. Now, we've received information that you and Miss Mason visited Carrie Adams the morning that she was brought in. Do you deny that?"

"No, that's certainly true."

"Why didn't Miss Mason tell us about it?"

"I don't know, sir. Maybe she didn't think that it was relevant for your case. I don't see how what we did could be related to the murder, but I admit that I don't know anything about police matters."

"Well, I hope you're not trying to be sarcastic. Tell us what happened. How did you happen to get involved?"

"Please, sir. I was working the night shift as the charge nurse in Ward 6. A little before 6:30, I got a call from Miss Mason asking if I could help her with the Admissions form for Carrie Adams. Since our ward was quiet, I said that I could come to her office."

"Isn't it strange that she would need help with something simple like that? How competent is your Nursing Director?"

"I think she's fantastic in her job. She said that she never had to fill out that form before. It's almost uncalled for that one of our nurses has to be the admitting official. In any event, once she saw the form all she had was a question about what to do because both Judge Welch and Dr. Carson had signed the committal papers."

"Okay, how did that get you involved with Carrie Adams?"

"After doing the paperwork, she was going to check on Miss Adams because she was comatose from drugs when she arrived. She asked me to accompany her because I work with the new admissions on our ward."

"I thought you said you work the night shift. What do you do, sing to your patients in their sleep?"

"No, sir. I was only on the night shift for two weeks while the normal charge nurse was on vacation. Because I'm not married, I can be pretty flexible. Now, I'm back on my regular day shift, working with Nancy Stewart, the charge nurse on Ward 6. Also, my assignments are a little more complex. I only work three days a week on the ward. The other sixteen hours are devoted to our outpatient clinic for wives and children who have been abused that I run under the supervision of Dr. Harvey."

Detective Perkins took over the questioning. "Matt, you're the one who's being sarcastic. Miss Hughes, tell me what happened when you got to the Violent Ward. Were you able to help the prisoner?"

"No, sir. I didn't have any interaction with her."

"Can you tell us about yourself?"

"I'm 28. I've worked at Elm Hill for seven years since I graduated from Nursing School. My parents and brothers live in Chicago. That's where I went to Nursing School, but I came here because of Elm Hill's reputation as a good psychiatric hospital. I like working with patients. I feel that I've been able to help many of them. Perhaps because I don't have children, I like to care for people. It's great when they can go home."

"Do you think Carrie murdered her father?"

"Yes, isn't that what all the evidence says?"

"Aren't you worried that she can avoid punishment by staying at Elm Hill? What about Judge Adams? Doesn't he deserve justice?"

"I won't argue with you, sir. I don't have any say about it."

"Well, for better or worse, neither do we.

"I'm sorry, Emma, but we have to ask you and Miss Mason a few more questions. Laura, would you please take her to the bathroom and then to the car. Also, ask Denise to have Miss Mason come in."

"Yes, sir. Here, Emma. I need to take your arm. Don't worry, it's just our procedure."

Miss Mason rose, whispered that we should stay there, and left. A few minutes later, we heard the door in the conference room open and Miss Mason brightly say, "Hello, Denise said that you wanted to see me."

"If you don't remember me, I'm Detective Perkins. We need to ask you and Emma some more questions away from here. Are you free to come with us now?"

"Are you arresting us? It sounds like I should have Dr. Rydberg call Jeremy Brown, our legal representative. Denise, could you please see Dr. Rydberg immediately if they're taking us away."

"No, you're not being put under arrest. We just want to have a chat where we're in control and get to know a little more about you."

Mrs. Holdstrom touched my shoulder and whispered, "Quick, we need to be back in my office."

Five minutes later, Miss Mason joined us in Mrs. Holdstrom's office.

"Hi, Gwen, Andy. How much did you hear?"

"We heard that they were going to question you someplace else but weren't arresting you. Then, I brought Andy here in case you came back. What do you think is happening?"

"I'm not sure, but I don't think they're planning anything too bad for us. Detective Perkins didn't object when I sent Denise to tell Dr. Rydberg what was happening and ask him to raise the roof if we're not back by seven. You notice that nobody escorted me back here like the policewoman took charge of Emma. Andy, would you mind coming with me? You know far more than either Emma or I about how Carrie is treated. Also, the more of us there are, the less likely they are to do anything. I don't think there's any danger. Everyone says that Perkins is honest and that he doesn't have high-level backers. He shouldn't try to push the envelope in handling us."

"I'm happy to help you, ma'am. I can't see how I've done anything wrong."

"Thanks so much, Andy. No you haven't done anything wrong. And certainly neither has Emma. They're trying to scare her. That's stupid because there's nothing she can tell them. However, given what happened when a nasty sergeant tried to arrest her to retaliate because she wouldn't go to bed with him, I'm pretty sure that they'll be very careful about going any further."

We went out the back of the hospital to get the car that was evidently reserved for the Director of Nursing and then pulled around to the front parking lot since, according to Miss Mason, we'd been asked to follow the policewoman's squad car. Detective Perkins, a short and stocky man in his early forties who looked to be in very good physical condition, waved to us and got into the front passenger's seat. Officer Sanders was driving with poor Emma in the cage behind the detective. Detective Kempton had evidently left already. As we drove down the hill and toward downtown, Miss Mason told me about how she had rescued Emma from the police. When we were still a little north of the downtown area, the police car turned left into Bud's Bar and Grill that advertised "Warm Beer and Slow Service" and drove to the back of the building. Miss Mason remarked, "So that's why they just didn't ask us to meet them at police headquarters."

We pulled up next to them. On the other side of their car, Detective Perkins got Emma out of the back and led her toward the back door of the building. The tall and light blond Office Sanders waited for us, smiled, said that she didn't want us to get lost, and led us through the kitchen and a short passage to a private room with a table that had a dozen chairs around it. The two detectives and Emma were already seated. The policewoman sat next to Emma. Miss Mason took the chair facing Detective Perkins, and I sat beside Officer Sanders, leaving the mean Detective Kempton by himself on the other long side of the table.

Detective Perkins then nodded to Miss Mason, "We thought we should have a conversation where nobody could hear or record us. This isn't a place that cops come to."

Suddenly, there was a loud clank of metal on wood. We all swiveled toward the sound and saw the policewoman trying to scoop her handcuffs back into her purse. Miss Mason broke the silence in a very sweet tone that Mrs. Holdstrom had warned was akin to the rattle of a rattlesnake.

"Are you threatening to arrest me, ma'am? Whatever for? Why did you drag poor Emma and Andy here? They're innocents, as you must well know. If you're going to handcuff me, please use mine that are padded." A set of leather covered cuffs slid in front of me toward the policewoman.

"I wasn't threatening you. I was just trying to get a handkerchief when they fell out. But you shouldn't be impeding Detective Perkins' investigation. He's a very good man and law enforcement officer."

Miss Mason responded, again sounding sweet and submissive. "I'm sorry that you feel that way, but I don't see how I've done anything wrong or impeded your investigation in any way. I know you think that

Carrie Adams is a murderess who should be having her head shaved for the electric chair. If sending her to Elm Hill was cheating justice, I don't see how we're to blame. She was committed by Judge Welch, who certainly doesn't have a reputation for coddling miscreants. Furthermore, we had our Admission nurses run tests and photograph her for you. Since you interrogated Emma just now, you must see some significance in our visit to the Violent Ward the morning that Carrie was brought in. I didn't mention it later that day because I couldn't see how anything that was happening in the hospital could be relevant to the murder. If you think differently, I'd be happy to tell you all that I know."

Detective Perkins interjected, trying to sound reasonable. "I agree with all you said, but what about the fact that we had to send Laura to jiggle her handcuffs at a laboratory worker at the Medical Center? We've also heard that there're lots of recording devices in your hospital. I bet it wouldn't take much investigation to find out that you've been spying on us."

Chapter 11 ~ Meeting of the Minds

Laura started to say something, but Detective Perkins held up his hand. "No, Miss Mason. We're not going to hassle you. You haven't done anything wrong. Please don't think badly of Laura. She certainly wasn't trying to intimidate you. She knows as well as you do that anyone who arrests one of you nurses without several unimpeachable witnesses would end up in a jail cell themselves. All of us here respect Emma for her work with abused wives and children. Matt actually apologized to her before you came in for getting too enthusiastic about playing a 'bad cop' to make Laura and I seem more sympathetic.

"However, we get the impression that you're doing some investigating yourself, which suggests that you don't think Carrie's guilty. Isn't that true?"

"I don't deny that I think there's some incongruous evidence. Is that bad? Aren't your investigations supposed to be about finding the truth?"

"I'm not sure whether Matt and Laura are mad that you're trying to prove Carrie's innocence. In any event, now let me shock my associates for real. I share your suspicion that Carrie may be innocent."

This certainly seemed to upset Officer Sanders. "Richard, what are you saying? I know you like to play games, but what about all the evidence against her? What else is there? What have you been hiding from Matt and me?"

Detective Perkins laughed heartily. "I haven't hidden anything, Laura. I just didn't want to challenge what all the big shots think without absolute proof. I didn't say anything to you and Matt for two reasons. I didn't want to influence your own judgments about the investigation or to put you on the spot if people asked what we were doing.

"Well, we're off duty now, or we'd have to write up what we're talking about which definitely would be a dangerous idea. Let me go order a couple of pitchers of beer. Miss Mason, your two people don't have anything to fear from us. Just like Emma considers some of her patients to be like her children, I'd guess that you feel that Emma and

Andy are like a daughter and son to you. I know if I saw a couple of bear cubs in the woods I'd walk away quickly and keep my gun cocked until I was well beyond any place that mama bear could be. Laura, why don't you relieve Miss Mason's fears that we were mistreating Emma while I order our refreshments? Tell her why you two were giggling like high school girls at my expense when we pulled up."

I turned to the young woman beside me, who suddenly didn't seem so intimidating, and asked if I could call her "Laura."

"Sure, Andy. You're Emma's friend. We're the three young ones here."

She then slid Miss Mason's handcuffs back to her. "Here, ma'am. Do you have to handcuff a lot of your patients?"

"No, Laura, at least not now. I got these when I worked in Downsville where a nurse often didn't have anyone to help or protect her. I also found that immediate restraint was the best way to calm patients who were becoming agitated or violent. There's a saying among psychiatric nurses that we should always stay calm and carry wrist restraints. When I came here as a charge nurse in the Violent Ward, I certainly kept them in my purse, but I only had to use them two or three times because attendants were almost always there to deal with manic or violent patients. Since I've been Director of Nursing for the last two years, they've just sifted down to the bottom of my handbag. Well, let's get back to a lighter interlude. What were you and Emma giggling about?"

"Richard was asking her about her work. She cares about her patients and work to make them better. But then she talked about all the notes she has to write up and how she's afraid that most of the bossy doctors don't pay much attention to the nurses who generally know more about the patients than they do. Then I said, 'doctors sound like detectives.' That gave us all the giggles, even Richard laughed."

We all laughed. Just then Detective Perkins came in followed by a barmaid carrying a tray with two pitchers of beer, a coke for Emma, and several bowls of peanuts. As we sipped our drinks, Detective Perkins began, "Miss Mason—"

She quickly interjected, "If you want to be friends, not enemies, let's be 'Carol' and 'Richard.'"

"That's an excellent idea, Carol, at least as long as there are no outsiders around. You're right that the police believe that Carrie killed her father and that they're only looking for evidence that supports that theory. In that environment, it would be stupid to argue the contrary unless you have an alternate solution signed, sealed, and delivered which, unfortunately, I'm a long way from having. Really, it's probably a blessing that she's at Elm Hill and out of danger of a speedy trial and conviction.

"As to the indications that she's not guilty, the first was obvious from the pictures that you gave us. There's no bruise on her shoulder where the shotgun would have given her a mighty kick. Why Sarah Harker didn't say anything about that is beyond me. The second comes from what little Carrie was able to tell us. Were you eavesdropping on us? Or, would you like to see a transcript?"

"Don't be coy, Richard. Did you find her fingerprints on the apron and rubber gloves by the sink?"

"Well, maybe you should be a detective. Yes, her prints were there. Even more conclusively, they weren't on the fresh dish towel that was hanging out but were on a dirty one in the hamper by the cellar stairs. Somebody obviously tossed the towel she had used and replaced it. Moreover, the refrigerator handle had been wiped clean and the eggnog container was gone. I can't think of an innocent reason for those things, especially since the housekeeper claimed that she hadn't done any of them. Also, the dishpan was totally dry. Since my divorce I've had enough experience to know that it wouldn't dry that completely so fast."

"That dovetails with my suspicions that Carrie could have been drugged by the eggnog. Earlier today I finally got a chance to talk to her alone for a moment. She said that, beyond what she told you, she remembers going into the kitchen, having her snack, washing up, and then being overcome with fatigue. I think that there was something in the eggnog that made her pass out and that the murderer then came in and gave her a strong dose of sodium amytal once she was unconscious. You might have noted that there were the marks of two injections on her arm, while the ambulance attendant only gave her one."

"That's great, Carol. The drug evidence is suggestive but less conclusive. While there were traces of powdered cocaine by the sink, there were no drugs at all in either Carrie's or Patty Renfro's rooms. Both my girls go to Osloville High and know Carrie a little. She's a clean-cut girl, who's a long way from acting like an addict."

"What do you think about the lab results that Laura frightened some poor girl into giving her?"

"Actually, I was just teasing you about the blood work. That's why Laura looked so puzzled. What happened was that one of the ambulance men let me know that he heard that a blood test had been done at the Medical Center for Elm Hill two days after the murder and that he had been quizzed about what sedation he had used that night. I figured that it was probably you who were doing some sleuthing, but that didn't upset me. If the results confirmed that Carrie was high on drugs, I could always demand them later. If they showed she was clean, they would set off a commotion that we don't need now and might even lead to somebody trying to fabricate contradictory evidence. Thus, I didn't do anything to follow up the tip."

"Well, Richard. We think alike. Incidentally, there were no drugs in her blood."

"I guess I should thank you, Carol. There's another piece of evidence that is problematic, but I don't know how to interpret it. Jimmy Clay, one of our smarter and more diligent officers, found a plastic raincoat with what looked like bloodstains on it buried in a garbage can outside the house the next morning. Since there was blood all over Carrie's dress, I couldn't figure out how the coat could fit in, so Jimmy and I put it in a bag quietly. Since Jimmy is friends with your Chief Attendant, Clem Jones, I wouldn't be surprised if you might know about this already."

"Actually, the information flow went the other way. When we were undressing Carrie, I noticed that the blood spatter on the front of the dress didn't continue upon her skin above it. That suggests that someone else may have worn the raincoat under the dress when they shot Judge Adams and then transferred the dress to Carrie's unconscious body. Consequently, I think that the coat is exculpatory. Clem actually called Jimmy early in the morning after the murder and asked him to be on the lookout for something that might substantiate my theory."

"Congratulations. Finally, let's get to something that makes me suspicious but may not have anything to do with the murder. We questioned Emma today because we got a tip from a cop, whom I don't respect very much, that you and she had tried to interfere with Carrie's treatment and that you had then brought Andy in to spy on the ward. I'm not sure what that meant. Were you making the murderer nervous? Or, did somebody just want to cause you some grief because of hospital politics? We certainly have lots of nasty stuff that goes on in the Police Department."

"Well, there's certainly something going on at the hospital, but I'm not sure that it is necessarily anything related to the murder. The Nurse Manager of the Violent Ward resents me for getting the Nursing Director's job that she wanted and is very protective about controlling her ward. Also, we just learned that some outside doctors who treat individual patients are trying to get power over the hospital administration. We'll certainly keep a keen eye out and let you know if anything relevant to your investigation crops up."

"Well, Carol, you've been forthright about what you're trying to do. Let me tell you something about us. We've got very strong personal ties, so we won't be playing any games with each other or with you. Matt and Laura are engaged to be married. Matt and I have worked together for ten years, and Laura is the sister of my ex-wife and something of my protégé."

On that happy note, we passed around the second pitcher of beer, congratulated Laura and Detective Kempton who now seemed much nicer, and turned the conversation to trivial matters. When we got up to leave, Miss Mason stepped around me to tell Laura something in a low voice that I couldn't hear, but I did catch the policewoman's response.

"That sounds like a good idea. Maybe we'll get something. Let me see if Richard will approve it."

On our way home, Miss Mason asked me what I thought about the police investigation. When I said that Detective Perkins seemed to be really on the ball, she smiled.

"Unless he's not telling us, Richard's ignoring something pretty suspicious at the crime scene."

However, when I asked her what it was. She just told me to be patient because she didn't want to point a finger at anyone without real proof.

Chapter 12 ~ The Maid's Tale

I found out what Miss Mason and the policewoman had been talking about the next afternoon. I had come up to Mrs. Holdstrom's office about 1:15 where we had starting chatting about her children. As this topic was winding down, her telephone rang. She listened for an instant and said, "Okay." She then had the switchboard connect her with Miss Mason. "The policewoman's here. She just came through the gate. Yes, I'll tell Andy to come in with her."

When I ushered Laura into Miss Mason's office, she motioned us to the conference table where a pot of coffee and an inviting plate of sweet rolls were sitting.

Laura started the conversation. "Hello, Miss Mason. Talking to the maid was a good idea. Richard asked me to bring you a copy of the tape and play it for you. She couldn't tell us anything about the murder, but what she did say does give us something more to think about."

"Thanks so much, Laura. I see you're wearing a belt with handcuffs dangling from them. Is that what Richard meant by 'jiggling your handcuffs?'"

"You don't miss anything, do you ma'am? Policewomen aren't always respected. Sometimes we have to be less than subtle about exerting our authority. I thought that a little hint might make the maid more willing to cooperate. Then I got so caught up in things that I forgot to take the cuffs off the belt.

"When I got to the Adams house, the cook, Mrs. Larson, answered the door. I asked for Patty. She said that she was cleaning bathrooms and went to get her. She returned pretty quickly with the girl. She was wearing her black maid's uniform, a white apron, yellow rubber gloves, and a red kerchief. When I asked if there was a place we could talk in private, Mrs. Larson nodded and took us to the Judge's law library in the back of the house. She hardly said anything, but I got the impression that she didn't have much good will for Patty, who looked subdued and even a little frightened. I set up the tape recorder and started the questioning. Here, let me play it for you now that we've all got coffee."

"Hello, Patty. I'm Officer Sanders. Do you remember me? I was one of the people who interviewed you the morning after the murder."

"Yes ma'am."

"Don't worry. We don't suspect you of the murder. Your alibi checked out completely. However, there's something else that came up. Do you know what you've been accused of?"

"I think so ma'am. Are you going to arrest me?"

"If you tell me the truth, you shouldn't be in any trouble, at least not legally. Also, why don't you take off your gloves and kerchief? They must be hot."

"Yes, ma'am."

"First, do you know anything about where Carrie got drugs?"

"You're wrong ma'am. I'm sure that Miss Adams wasn't doing anything bad."

"Didn't she fight with her parents over her drug use?"

"Her mother got colder toward her this spring, but there weren't any big fights. I'm not in her social class by a long shot, but we were the only two young people in the house. We confided in each other a lot. Even a couple of days before the murder, she was happy and feeling normal."

"What about guns? Did she know how to use them?"

"I'm pretty sure that she didn't."

"What about you, Patty. We've heard a claim that you were supplying drugs to Carrie."

"That's not true. It's a lie! Please, ma'am."

"Would you be willing to take blood and urine tests to prove that you're not a drug abuser?"

"Yes ma'am. I'll to do anything to prove I'm innocent. Please, ma'am. I certainly know how bad drugs are."

Here, Laura stopped the tape. "Can you do the tests? Richard thinks that unless she turns out positive, which is doubtful, it might be a good idea to keep the samples away from police headquarters since we don't want to look like we're gathering exculpatory evidence. Also, as you'll soon see, she might benefit from some psychiatric counseling. She's pretty broken up."

After Miss Mason said she'd be happy to help, Laura restarted the tape machine.

"Now, Patty, we need to move on to something that's bound to be painful."

"I know, ma'am."

"Were you having an affair with Judge Adams? Is that why Mrs. Adams hates you now?"

"Yes ma'am. Can I go to jail?"

"No. There may be some old law on the books somewhere, but I've never heard of anyone being prosecuted for adultery. If they started doing that, we'd probably need a lot more jails and prisons. Now tell me about yourself and how this started."

"Yes, ma'am. I had to drop out of high school when I was a sophomore because my dad died and we needed more money. I got a job as a waitress at the Fireside Diner, but our family's situation was still pretty tight. The Diner certainly isn't a classy restaurant, but Judge Adams came in once or twice a month for lunch because he was friends with the owner, so we got to know each other. About two years ago, his maid quit to get married. He then offered the job to me. He said that the pay was a little less, but I would get full room and board. I took the job because I could still give Mum some money for my younger brother and sister, save her the cost of feeding me, and end having to share a bedroom with my bratty twelve-year old sister. For about a year things went well. Then just when I broke up with my boyfriend, I noticed that Judge and Mrs. Adams were getting colder toward each other. Carrie noticed it, too, and started to worry.

"The affair started almost by accident. If we hadn't been alone that evening, I don't think anything would have happened. Judge Adams made a special arrangement for us servants for last Thanksgiving. On Thanksgiving Day, I got off to spend it with my family, while I looked after the three Adams for the rest of the weekend so the Larsons, the housekeeper and the butler, could visit her brother and his family in Farmdale. On Friday, we had an early dinner because Mrs. Adams and Carrie were going to a concert. After washing up, I took a glass of cognac into the law library where Judge Adams was working. I put the glass down. He thanked me for being thoughtful and said that it should make him feel better. He looked so sad that I bent down, rubbed his shoulders, and kissed him on the check. Then I started to cry because I thought I'd be fired. Instead, he kissed me through my tears. I wasn't a blushing virgin so I took him up to my room so we wouldn't leave a mess where anyone would find it.

"After that we made love every week or two. I don't think that anyone suspected anything until recently. Then about ten days before the murder, Mrs. Adams came to my room after my work was done for the day. She grabbed my hair and forced me to kneel in front of her while she sat on the bed. In a low voice, filled with hate, she called me a wicked slut. She asked if I thought I could steal her husband and her house. I cried a little and said no. She demanded to know if I were leading Carrie into bad ways, and I just cried. She said that she'd love to throw me out on the street, but that would just expose the scandal and humiliate her. After the murder, she called me in, in front of the Larsons, and said that she was stuck with me to preserve her husband's good name and that if I tried to leave, she'd make sure that I'd never get another job and that our family would starve."

Laura stopped the tape. "Well, this is something more to think about. There were tensions in the house, but the wife clearly didn't pull the trigger.

"I'm so glad you thought of this, Miss Mason. I felt like a real detective when I was interviewing her. Usually, I just escort women shoplifters to jail. That's a long way from being Nancy Drew."

This piqued my curiosity since I didn't think that I remembered seeing policewomen, even in College City. So, I asked her what they did. This made her smile.

"It's too bad that we're so invisible. They're two of us on each shift in case the patrolmen or detectives need help with female prisoners or victims. As I just mentioned, our biggest duty involves shoplifters whenever the stores have a crackdown. The men don't want our help with prostitutes, of course. Really, I'd like to go to more 'family war' calls. Many beat cops are too lenient toward drunken bums who beat up their wives. That's why I'm so excited about this case because I'm working full time with a detective team."

Chapter 13 ~ Judge Adams & Jenny

A week and a half later after a lazy Friday, on which my major activity was taking the bus to downtown Osloville for an afternoon of exploring, I went in for my first weekend shift on Saturday morning and immediately realized that I was in a dicey political situation. Miss Rayburn had evidently decided that our three most dangerous patients, Carrie, Mean Monica, and Jenny Sachs, needed greater security and supervision. In particular, she wanted them to be individually escorted when they were out of their cells, such as during the "parade." Previously, Amy had handled both Carrie and Jenny. During their exercise or parade, she had walked a straitjacketed Carrie, while Jenny had been placed in a restraining belt and tethered to the other women who were being exercised. The new, stricter rules, however, meant that different aides had to be in charge of each of them. For unspecified reasons, Miss Rayburn assigned Jenny to me and transferred Mrs. Smith, my "un-messy" patient, to Amy. Rather than making Amy happy that she now had one less troublesome patient, losing control over Jenny appeared to enrage her. Mrs. Greene got upset as well perhaps, as Carly speculated, because she wasn't pleased to have Amy in a nasty mood.

After having an unexpectedly brief chat with my other two patients, I went to Jenny's room. She was in her early thirties and was probably the neatest patient on the ward. She was sitting almost primly on her bed but looked quite startled when I came in.

"Hello, Mrs. Sachs. I'm Andy Russell. I'll be taking care of you on this shift now. The Nurse Manager wants you to be individually escorted when you leave your room, so Miss Strong can't care for both you and Carrie Adams anymore. By the way, do you prefer to be called Mrs. Sachs or Jenny?"

"Hello, Mr. Russell. Call me Jenny. The other staff do. In addition, I really don't like to hear my ex-husband's name."

After breakfast, Mrs. Strickland and Miss Peters wanted to spend the morning in the day room, the first time that both had wanted to do this while I was caring for them. It was longer than I expected before I cleared away Jenny's breakfast and got her ready for her exercise period. She meekly held her hands on her head while I got the restraining belt locked around her waist and then allowed me to buckle her wrists into the straps that were attached to the belt. Then she sat on her bed and held up her legs so I didn't have to kneel down to attach her leg straps. After I complimented her on being so cooperative, her reply was a little sad.

"Miss Strong has made sure that I learned how to behave over the last eight months. Really, this is so much more comfortable than the strait jacket I had to wear for my first year that I wouldn't do anything that would justify stronger restraints. Furthermore, since I'm a homicidal maniac, the other patients and the staff wouldn't stand for me running around loose. Being restrained may help me, then, because I can't be blamed for anything."

"You don't look like a homicidal maniac. You seem much calmer and more in control of yourself than the patients on this ward."

"As you probably heard, I stabbed my husband in a fit of uncontrollable rage. I'm normal almost all the time, but I feel so frustrated in here sometimes that even I know that it could happen again."

Once we started walking around the ward, it was easy to get her talking about herself. Her long isolation, I would guess, made a friendly ear very attractive.

"Thank you for listening and caring Mr. Russell. I'm here because I fell in love with the wrong man. My white knight and saint turned out to be a demon.

"I come from a prosperous business family in the state capital. I was supposed to go to college and find a suitable husband. I went to St. Catherine's in 1943 and majored in English literature. I was an average student, but I enjoyed academics. Then my life was transformed in the spring of 1947 by a visit to campus by Rodney Sachs, a war hero and Assistant Secretary of State in Governor Marsh's administration. He gave a wonderful speech about the great future that America had in store and about how government through programs like the G.I. Bill had opened up new opportunities for our people. I was impressed and even impassioned. Though my parents were from the wealthy business class, I had always felt that the New Deal had saved the nation from ruin. Tell me Mr. Russell, are you interested in politics?"

"Not that much. My parents run a drug store in a small rural town and before the Great Depression used to like Progressive Republicans because they protected small farmers from greedy railroads and corporations. Our community depended, and still does for that matter, on the farmers, and my parents had many good friends who were farmers. Once the Depression hit, the New Deal helped a lot of farmers in our area. I'm not really attached to one party. Maybe, I'll become more interested now that I can vote. What happened with you and Mr. Sachs? It's a long way from listening to a guy's speech to getting married to him."

"One of my government professors who was politically active got me a clerical job in Mr. Sachs' office when I graduated that June. My parents had mixed feelings about this. On the one hand, they thought that the job was beneath someone of my class, and they didn't have much use for Democrats of any stripe. On the other, they also thought that I might be getting a good chance to meet politically powerful people. I found that the job was pretty routine, but it still was exciting because we were in the middle of inside news and political gossip. I guess I kept making moon eyes at Mr. Sachs because he starting making small talk and sometimes staring at me. I think that I was pretty good looking then. Also, it probably made him feel good that someone fifteen years younger was attracted to him.

"The first time that anything physical happened was at the office Christmas party where quite a few of us had too much eggnog with rum. As I was leaving, he asked me to come into a side office for a moment. He didn't even shut the door, but as soon as we were out of sight, he kissed me, patted my bottom, and told me I was his good girl. I quickly left, feeling both scared and excited. Nothing more happened between us until the next March when he called the whole staff together for a momentous announcement on March 15, a Monday I think, perhaps to commemorate the Ides of March. Everyone was sure that Governor Marsh was going to lose the upcoming 1948 election. Those of us who had political, not permanent, jobs were starting to get nervous. Mr. Sachs said he was resigning his position at the end of the week because the Democrats under Harry Truman were betraying the interests of the American people. He said that the Secretary of State had promised that any of us who wanted to stay could keep our jobs and that he was pretty sure that he could find jobs for anyone who wanted to come with him to work on the campaign of Thomas Rutland, the Republican candidate for Governor. His two top political aides immediately said that they would join him. I'm pretty sure that they had known what was going to happen. Nobody else said anything because almost everyone was a loyal Democrat.

"Later in the day, I went to his office and asked if I could go with him. He laughed and said that he was sure that he could get a better job for me. Then he told me to come around his desk. The next thing that I knew, he pulled me onto his lap, kissed me long and sexily, and began to fondle my breasts. Initially I was shocked, but then just as I was starting to enjoy it his secretary Judy burst in and screamed, 'You vile slut. You'll ruin his reputation.' He held me for another minute until I calmed down a little and then told me that I should take paid vacation for the rest of the week and then go see Jennifer at the Rutland campaign headquarters the following Monday. I left the office in tears, realizing that my life had changed and that now I would face the humiliation of political gossip. Oh, Mr. Russell, I see from your watch that it's time to go back. I guess that we'll need another day or two for you to understand why I'm here and how I'm treated."

Amy pigeonholed me as I was leaving lunch to gather the trays of my three patients who had to eat in their cells. Instead of her hostility of the morning, she was now expressing concern for my wellbeing, but I have to admit that I questioned her sincerity.

"Well, Andy. I see that you've survived a morning with that nasty Jenny Sachs."

"She seemed pretty docile to me."

"Don't be stupid. You can see that you haven't worked with her long. She's almost as dangerous as Carrie Adams. She tried to murder our Secretary of State. She attacked me twice. Threats are the only thing that works with her. I told her that she'd be gagged if she tried to bite me. Take my advice and treat her like a biting dog. At the first sign of agitation, don't just grab her arm. Give her a hammer lock, force her to her knees, and call Thomas."

"Well, she did say that you had taught her how to behave."

"That shows that you need to be strict with her. Just pray that she doesn't realize how weak you are."

When I went to retrieve her lunch tray, I asked Jenny how Miss Strong had treated her. She looked a little wary and just said that Miss Strong was quite strict. Given the demeaning way in which Amy treated Carly and me, I decided to keep an open mind about what Jenny was really like. The next day, Jenny was again submissive and eager to begin her story.

"Well, you heard about my dramatic exit from the Secretary of State's Office yesterday. If I had gone home then, I think that my life would have been conventional and that I wouldn't be here, locked up for the rest of my life. I can't even have books because I'm considered so dangerous.

"When I left his office with Judy glaring at me as I passed her desk, I didn't know what to think. I wasn't that experienced. I'd necked and petted in college, but I was still a virgin. I guess I loved Mr. Sachs, but I'd never imagined that I'd have an affair with him. I wondered at that time if Judy was like that, too, and whether that was why she hated me.

"Mrs. Sachs divorced him in June but didn't mention anything about sexual impropriety. Instead, she circulated the story that he had married her when he came home from the war because she was the niece of Governor Marsh and that, when he decided that it was advantageous to switch parties shortly after New Year's, he became cold and even abusive toward her. He didn't contest her, and the divorce went through pretty quickly. He didn't say more than a few words at a time when he saw me, which wasn't that often, until after the election was over. Mr. Rutland won easily and appointed Mr. Sachs his Secretary of State. Once the election was over and my job with the campaign staff ended, I moved back in with my parents. My two younger brothers had both gone away to college by this time, so I think they were a little lonely. Then, starting in early December, Mr. Sachs began asking me out to discrete dinners every week or two. When he took me home, he kissed me hard, but that was all. Almost out of the blue he asked me to marry him on March 15th and set our wedding date for New Year's Day 1950 to commemorate the second half of the twentieth century.

"I was so happy during the time between the proposal and the wedding. My parents liked him much better now that he was a Republican. While nothing was ever said to me directly, I got the impression that dad and his business associates were glad to have a friend as Secretary of State after sixteen years of Democratic administrations. Conversely, Mr. Sachs probably benefitted from new business backing as well. Certainly, my time in the Secretary of State's Office had exposed me to the importance of mutual favors in politics."

"So far everything seems to have worked out for you, Jenny. What went wrong?"

"We had a wonderful six months of marriage, but after that things went downhill pretty quickly. We had a large wedding and then went to Bermuda for two weeks which was a treat since there had just been a blizzard here. Our first few months together were heaven. We talked about his office and how well his reorganization was going, and I went to many political and civic functions with him. I was so proud of him. He said he loved me because I was so intelligent. By May or June, however, I started to notice some change in how he was treating me. He became more distant, didn't like to chat with me as much, and started attending a lot of functions by himself. What got me worried was that he became much less romantic. In early June, he moved me into a separate bedroom because, he said, our sleeping schedules were so different. After that we didn't make love very much. When we did, he was no longer tender and caring. I think it wasn't until early fall when I realized what had happened. I went to his office to see if he would like to go out to lunch in a nearby restaurant that we had enjoyed together in the past. I hadn't been to his office since March and hoped that a happy surprise might make him interested in me again. How wrong I was. When I walked into his outer office, I saw that his previous chief secretary had been replaced by Judy. When she looked up and saw me, she smiled at me with gloating eyes. I went to the closest powder room and cried for fifteen minutes.

"For the next two-and-a-half years I felt so alone. Our family is a devoutly religious one, so divorce seemed out of the question. I couldn't tell even my parents or my brothers because that would add to my shame. We drifted apart, which was tolerable for a while. Then in early 1952, he started being mean to me, probably hoping that I'd agree to a divorce and to taking responsibility for it. He made demeaning remarks to me when other people were about and yelled at me in private, calling me stupid and clumsy. Even the servants, who had been cold to me because of their loyalty to his first wife, started showing sympathy for me. It came to a head during a party that we hosted to celebrate the Republican sweep in the 1952 elections. During the party, which my parents hadn't been able to attend, thank heaven, he mocked me for being a radical Democrat who wanted to help the little people when I came to him out of college. Then after everyone left, he followed me into the kitchen, told me in front of the servants that he had always worn a condom with me because he didn't want me to be the mother his children, and demanded a divorce. A wave of hate engulfed me. I grabbed up a long kitchen knife and stabbed him. I don't think I was aiming anywhere, but, thank heaven I only hit him in the shoulder.

"Oh, Mr. Russell, look at the time. You need to get me back to my cell. Anyway, I need to stop now. I'm getting too emotional."

What had struck me about Jenny by now was, Amy to the contrary, how coherent she was and how logically she thought, unlike almost all our other patients on the Violent Ward. The next morning, Monday, she was again very cooperative and submissive. In preparation for her temperature taking, she had untied the bottom string on her prison-striped hospital gown and was stretched out on her tummy with her wrists and ankles by the bed restraints. As I buckled her down, she thanked me for being so gentle and caring with her and said that she was pretty sure that she wouldn't get emotional today.

Unlike Saturday and Sunday, she didn't start talking immediately when I took her out for her exercise period. Rather, we walked almost five minutes before she was ready to conclude her story.

"I made the headlines. My parents were shocked, but after they visited me in jail, they said that he was a monster and that they would do everything in their power to protect me. I became a real political football. On the one hand, the Governor and many Republican leaders wanted me crucified for attacking one of the state's 'most distinguished leaders.' On the other, many business leaders quietly supported me, though nobody openly talked about how he had treated me. The Democrats, for their part, just laughed at a Republican scandal and at the claims of some Republicans that I was a radical socialist. The idea of sending me to Elm Hill originated from my father, but it was accepted by my husband and his political allies pretty quickly. They realized that continuing scandal and headlines would hurt the party and that, since Dad had hired an expensive and aggressive defense lawyer for me, some less than flattering things were likely to come out about Rodney at a trial. Indeed, his first wife offered to testify on my behalf and was quite sympathetic when she came to see me, especially after I assured her that I wasn't the one who had stolen him from her.

"In the end, I agreed to divorce him and to plead guilty to attempted murder for which I was sentenced to ten years in the women's penitentiary pending my treatment for criminal insanity. This was, according to the prosecution, to prevent liberal doctors from proclaiming me 'cured.' My Dad also agreed to having Dr. Simon Rust be my psychiatrist. He was supposedly the leading expert on the criminally insane in the state. Perhaps he had some connection to my husband or his cronies. In any event, he prescribed a very strict regimen for me. I had to been restrained at night, which meant I had to be put in diapers, wear a strait jacket whenever I was out of my cell, and undergo a strip search after seeing visitors. He visited me once a month but didn't seem very interested in anything I said.

"This went on for over six months. Then, from what I was told later by Miss Mason who was a charge nurse on the Violent Ward at that time, my treatment was reported at a Board of Directors meeting by Dr. Rydberg. Judge Adams, who was on the Board, got upset and asked whether it was usual to be so harsh to a patient. Three months later at another Board meeting, Miss Mason and Miss Rayburn reported that strict security had been imposed by Dr. Rust because of my violent insanity. At the time they had no reason to question it. However, over the almost nine months that I had been confined, I hadn't had one violent outburst, which was almost unprecedented for the permanent patients on the Violent Ward.

"Based on this report, Judge Adams issued a judicial order removing me from the care of Dr. Rust. The hospital then transferred me to Dr. Carson. He saw me weekly and at least seemed to listen to what I was saying. The strip searches and straitjacketing stopped, though I was still put in a restraining belt when I was outside my room. Another big improvement was that I was allowed to have books in my room and to sit in the day room as long as I was confined to iron anklets. This made things much more bearable. Indeed, I was starting to enjoy my life a little. I know I'll be here the rest of my life and never be able to have children. If I leave, I'll be taken straight to prison. I know I couldn't face that. The matrons in the State Capital Jail told me what the other prisoners and guards would do to a *stuck up rich bitch*."

"I'm so sorry for you, Jenny."

"Thank you, Mr. Russell. It wasn't so bad, but then it got much worse again once Miss Strong was hired as a nurses' aide and put in charge of me. She said that I had to be controlled better because my awful violent crime showed that I was totally unpredictable. At least she didn't reinstitute straitjacketing, but she put leg straps on for my exercise period, began more extensive strip searching than even when I first came here, stopped my use of the day room, allowed me to have reading materials only from ten to two, and threatened night time restraints again if I caused the least bit of trouble."

On this somber ending, I took her back to her room and removed her restraints. She smiled at me a little shyly and thanked me for being so kind to her. When I brought her lunch, I asked her what happened to the books that she used for her mid-day reading, and she said that Miss Strong had brought them at ten and taken them away at two.

Chapter 14 ~ Judge Adams & Mrs. Ward

The next day, Miss Mason asked me to help with one of the patients in another ward. "Andy, I don't have that much for you to do at present. Could you help with one of our elderly patients on Ward 2? She's Mrs. Betty Ward who was committed here by her children for senile dementia because she could no longer take care of herself. Her eyesight is fading and she's asked for someone to read to her. Unfortunately, most of the patients on that ward require so much attention that they can't spare anyone for extended reading. If you could give her an hour or two a day, I'm sure that she'll be very grateful. She's lonely, and I know that she wants someone to talk to."

"That's something I'll enjoy. When do you want me to start?"

"Well my clock is just about ready to strike two. Why don't you go up to Ward 2 and introduce yourself to her? Ask for Christine Maxwell, the charge nurse. She's expecting you."

Later I asked Mr. Jones about this assignment. His advice was slightly enigmatic, however. "I think you'll like Mrs. Ward. I'm glad she's getting more attention. However, while she didn't say anything, I think that Miss Mason wants you to keep your ears open."

When I got to Ward 2, I had to ring the bell by the door because I had a key only to my ward. I was let in by a quiet female attendant with gray hair. She took me back to the nurses' station and introduced me to Christine Maxwell, the charge nurse, who seemed to be in her early fifties with a plain but kindly face.

"Hello, Andy. Thank you so much for coming. It will be nice to have a young person on the ward. We don't have many, but there are a few who like to take care of the elderly. You'll see a lot of our patients just sitting around. They're not necessarily depressed like the ones on the Violent Ward would be. They're just tired or confused from their dementia. Actually, most of our staff like working here. They feel that they're helping nice people have the best quality of life possible.

"I'm so glad that you're willing to work with Mrs. Ward. Despite her dementia, she's still pretty sharp. She's losing her eyesight, so having somebody read her favorite books to her should pick up her spirits. Also, because there isn't that much sociability on the ward, she'd probably love to have a new friend even for an hour or two a day."

She then took me into the dayroom where I quickly noticed there weren't any benches or chairs with iron anklets. Mrs. Maxwell was right in that there wasn't much movement or conversation, even though I assumed that these elderly ladies had just finished their after-lunch naps. We went up to a woman with white curly hair and large spectacles, whose blue dress, stockings, and shoes looked quite respectable. She was gazing out the window and seemingly enjoying the sunny day that had not yet reached summer heat. She looked up at us more cogently than several other people in the dayroom had when we passed and seemed glad that I had come.

"Are you Andy Russell? Thank you for coming to cheer up an old lady. I really appreciate it. Thank you, too, Mrs. Maxwell for making it happen. Tell me a bit about yourself, Andy. I'm getting lonesome for the real world beyond this ward."

I gave a quick history of who I was and how I'd come to Elm Hill. She asked questions about my family and friends. As this conversation wound down, she asked if I could read to her for a few minutes before I left. When I nodded yes, she picked up a copy of *Little Women* that was bound in beautiful brown leather. I had never read it, so I was interested. We read the first chapter which, she said, brought back many pleasant memories from when she first read it as a high school student.

I had decided that asking Amy for the two books that Jenny had been reading was likely to provoke a major battle that might lead to greater restrictions on the poor patient. After I said good bye to Mrs. Ward and went off duty, I went by my room to change clothes and then rode the bus downtown. I visited a drugstore, which reminded me of my dad's, for the treat of an ice cream sundae and then went to the bookstore on Main Street where I got Jane Austin's *Pride and Prejudice* for Jenny. It was her favorite book and I also treated myself to a couple of murder mysteries as light reading.

I took *Pride and Prejudice* to Jenny as soon as I got to the Violent Ward the next morning, showing up for work twenty minutes early so that neither Amy nor Thomas would see the book. She was almost gleeful when I handed it to her and thanked me profusely. When we left for her exercise period, she said that she was talked out and asked me to tell her about the outside world. I kept her entertained with stories about movie stars, the popularity of President Eisenhower, and what growing up in a small town had been like for me. Then I asked if she wanted to hear some political news that might upset her.

"I can guess. Rodney is going to run for Governor because Mr. Rutland can't have a third consecutive term. Don't worry about upsetting me. My parents, who can visit me once a month, won't tell me anything about him, not even whether he married that sneaking and scheming Judy. I hate him, of course, but I truthfully don't care."

After writing up my nurse's notes, I went directly to Ward 2. Mrs. Ward was in the same chair. After we exchanged hellos, I read to her from *Little Women* for an hour and became increasingly fascinated by the March girls. When we took a break from the reading, I asked her to tell me about herself. Surprisingly, she looked a little sad.

"For most of my life, I was blessed and happy. Now at the end, it's not so good. This book takes me back to happier and more innocent days. It's easy to tell you about most of my life, but when we get through that, you can pick whether you want the official or unofficial version of the last two years.

"I was born in 1878 in New York State. My father owned a shoe store in Rochester which gave our family a good living. I loved school, especially reading. I was first introduced to *Little Women* when I was a freshman in high school. It made me realize that life would be more complex than I had naively assumed before then. I also fell in love with Robert, the son of a banker, during high school. After high school, he went to Columbia University, and I went to what's politely termed a 'finishing school' in New York City. We got engaged in his junior year and were married three days after his graduation.

"He had planned to go to work in the bank where his father was Vice-President in Rochester. However, a few months before his graduation, he received an intriguing offer. A friend of his father who had moved to Chicago a few years previously went into partnership with a businessman from State Capital to found the Osloville Bank here. They were looking for well-trained go-getters, and his father's friend thought of Robert. They offered him the position of loan officer with the opportunity for promotion to a manager's position if things went well. If Robert didn't like it, he could always go back to his dad's bank.

"Robert and I were both adventuresome and attracted to the idea of rapid promotion in a new bank, especially since we wouldn't lose anything if things didn't work out. Also, coming from Rochester, we weren't intimidated by snow and icy winds. It turned out that our decision to move here was rewarded almost immediately. Osloville was expanding in the early twentieth century, so there was lots of potential business for the new bank at a time when the other three local banks were poorly run. The partners, Mr. Brooks and Mr. Compton, were skilled bankers, who made the Osloville Bank the most respected and largest one in town within five years. Robert prospered as well. He took to banking as a duck takes to water. He had a good background in the profession from his father, and he was good with people. He also had an extremely good business sense. He could figure out which businesses were likely to succeed, both because they fit into the economic needs of the community and because their owners knew what they were doing. Within three years, Robert was the top manager in the bank below Mr. Brooks and Mr. Compton.

"We had also become part of what was called 'society' in the city. Certainly, Osloville in the early twentieth century did not have many rich or sophisticated people, but also there was no snobbery of old wealth against the up-and-coming. Because Robert was rising rapidly in the bank and working with many of the business leaders in town, we soon were socially engaged. Robert became special friends with Samuel Adams, the leading lawyer in town. We even became godparents to his son Daniel, the judge who was just murdered. We had our two children then: Kenneth in 1906 and Meredith in 1908.

"The first third of the twentieth century was a very good time in Osloville, except for the Griggs gang that got so powerful during Prohibition. Right after World War I, we built a beautiful home on River Ridge Road, just four houses away from our best friends, the Adams family. Our one little heartache, although we didn't think of it that way at the time, was that our son went to work for Osloville Bank's major rival in the late 1920s, First National, when he came home from college. He said that he wanted to make it on his own. Once he brought it up,

Robert felt that having an independent career might be good for him. He became friends with a loan manager at the bank, Gene Simmons, who soon was going out with Meredith and who then married her after a two-year courtship. The Great Depression brought terrible times to Osloville. Both Osloville Bank and First National were strong enough and smart enough to survive, though the other four banks in the county quickly vanished. While our income fell drastically, we had savings in the bank and were quite financially secure. Ironically, perhaps, since I'm now confined here, Robert put a good deal of work into helping Judge Adams and Mayor Stockville with their Elm Hill project. He was proud of contributing to it. It helped the city at the depths of the Depression and provided more humane treatment for women who were mentally ill. Of course, we then prospered along with many others when the Depression ended.

"Growing old can probably never end well. Robert and I loved each other and enjoyed each other throughout our marriage. He died of a massive heart attack in 1952. Perhaps that was a quick and easy way to go. He was laughing with Meredith's two sons just that morning. I was in shock and then grieved for a long time. Even after I accepted his death, the world was a lot darker. Now comes the point where my perceptions differ significantly from court and Elm Hill records. Which would you like to hear?"

"Why don't you start with the official version? Then we can decide whether I'm ready to hear the unofficial one."

"That sounds prudent, Andy. Maybe instead of a scholar, you should be a politician or a psychiatrist. Come on, smile. That was meant to be a joke.

"Clearly, I was depressed after Robert's death, but nobody seemed to think that that was strange until a little more than a year later. Then suddenly, in April 1953, Kenneth and Meredith raised the issue that I was no longer mentally competent to handle my own affairs and demanded that I give Kenneth power of attorney over all my assets and move into Dohlman's Nursing Home, which isn't a particularly nice one. When I resisted, they had the servants testify before Judge Welch, who committed me to Downsville for senile dementia and had me put under the care of a local psychiatrist, Dr. Carmichael. I called Judge

Adams who was appalled. He couldn't do anything about the declaration of mental incompetency, but by threatening legal action he forced an agreement where I was sent here with my husband's estate paying the fees. Thus, I've been in this ward for the last two years."

"Well, you imply that you have a much different view of these events. I'd certainly been happy to listen."

"You promise you won't tattle to Dr. Carmichael? I don't want him putting more restrictions on me."

"I promise. I don't even know him. I may have seen him in the Violent Ward, but if so it didn't register. He isn't treating any of the patients I care for there. Anyway, as I've told you, I'm just here for the summer."

"I may have been depressed, but I certainly don't think I was or am *gaga*. Shortly before he demanded to take over my financial assets and move me to a low-cost nursing home, I overheard a conversation between Kenneth and that slimy Gene Simmons over some great investment opportunity that could make them millionaires. I didn't think any more about it until I was here for six months, but they could have just been trying to grab my money. In addition, when I came into his care, Dr. Carmichael had a new eye doctor examine me, and the glasses he prescribed seemed to make my sight worse, not better."

"Did you talk about this to Judge Adams?"

"No, as I said, I didn't think there was anything sinister until well after my situation was settled. Then I was afraid that raising these issues would make me look paranoid. The only reasons I'm telling you this are that you're an outsider and that I'm afraid again of what might happen now that poor Judge Adams is dead."

I stopped by Mrs. Holdstrom's office on my way out of the hospital and told her what Mrs. Ward had said about Judge Adams. Before I went into specifics, I asked if Miss Mason might get her in trouble with Dr. Carmichael for complaining. She laughed and said that after we heard what Dr. Carmichael was trying to do to the hospital, Miss Mason would probably support any complaints against him even if they were clearly delusional.

The next day Jenny was overjoyed. She had left *Pride and Prejudice* out on her desk, but nobody from either the evening or night shifts seemed to notice or complain. She gave me her mother's telephone number so I could call her to ask for some of the books that she had loved in high school and college. After lunch, I spent most of my time with Mrs. Ward reading to her from *Little Women*. Our shared secret brought us together.

When I saw Miss Mason later in the day, she passed on some good news. "Regarding Mrs. Ward, it's unfortunately true that somebody with an unscrupulous lawyer has a good chance to abuse the elderly. Nothing worse should happen to her now, though. I called Jeremy Brown, who's now the senior partner in Adams, Brown, and Morris. He called back just after lunch to say that he personally reviewed the file and is willing to put the firm's resources and prestige on the line to protect Mrs. Ward. He also got an assurance from Judge Welch that he would refuse to permit altering the current situation."

That Saturday evening I got a special treat in the form of having dinner with Mr. Jones. His wife was working late at a formal dinner party, and his two children were out on dates. Since we really hadn't had a chance to visit since I'd arrived, we decided that fried chicken with peas and macaroni and cheese in the Elm Hill cafeteria provided a better meal than pot roast on River Ridge. He was curious about Mrs. Ward and nodded his head sagely when I told him her story.

"Ella always said that there was something wrong about sending Mrs. Ward here. She was a very nice lady and certainly seemed to be in control of all her facilities as far as the folks on River Ridge could see."

I then asked him about himself and how he had come to Elm Hill.

"My family comes from the South, but after Jim Crow laws were introduced at the turn of the century, they headed north to Chicago where the economy was booming. I was born in 1912 and met Ella in seventh grade. We've been sweethearts ever since. Her folks were chauffer and housekeeper to a businessman's family who moved up to Osloville in 1929 right after Ella and I graduated from high school. When she got there, Ella got a job as a secretary in a department store and found me a job in the store as a sales clerk, which was a polite way of saying that it was time to get married. A couple of years into the Depression, the store collapsed. To help us out, Ella's parents retired so that we could take their place.

"My big break came with the WPA program to build Elm Hill. I worked on the construction of the hospital and then got a job as an attendant when the hospital opened in 1938. Within three years I got promoted to Chief Attendant. In the process, I found out that I have good leadership and organizational skills. It was great working at the hospital. Almost everybody wanted to make sure that our patients were well cared for. In fact, we took pride in how much better than Downsville our facility was. Really, coming to Osloville has been a godsend for Ella and me. We've had good lives, and our kids should have better ones. We're really proud of them."

"You said that your daughter wants to go to Nursing School. Is it here or at Osloville Medical Center? "Would you like her to become another Miss Mason?"

"She'll definitely go to Elm Hill where we know that she'll be treated right. She's not as intelligent or as driven as Miss Mason, but then it's hard to think of many people who are. We hope that she'll be like Emma Hughes, a really nice and competent person who takes good care of her patients and enjoys doing so."

As we were concluding our meal with some apple pie, I asked him what Miss Mason might have meant by a clue from the night of the murder. He considered a moment and then was as enigmatic as she had been.

"She hasn't confided in me, but just think what happened that might not make sense."

Somehow, this made think that he might be a good detective, too, even if no light bulb went off in my head.

Chapter 15 ~ Embezzlement

The next Monday started a two-week cycle for which our shift worked Monday through Friday again. I was going to take the coming Friday and the following Monday and Tuesday off for our long graduation weekend and then make up for it by working three evenings on the night shift. While a hectic schedule, working forty hours a week was actually far less than I did at State U. Moreover, now that I was at Elm Hill I had no chores or preparations when I wasn't on duty. I also came to work on Monday with a decidedly mixed set of feelings. I was excited about my sister's and my graduations but at least a little reluctant to leave Elm Hill when so much was going on. The Adams murder was certainly proving to be much more exciting than I could have imagined, but it was also getting scary with the political undercurrents at the hospital. Finally, I was starting to wonder whether my job was making me focus on a few "trees" in the treatment of the mentally ill, while making the "forests" of abnormal psychology and psychiatric hospitals less visible.

After breakfast on Monday, Mrs. Holdstrom called down and told me to come to her office after writing up my nurse's notes rather than visiting Mrs. Ward. When I got to her office about 1:15, she seemed a little tense and took me into Miss Mason's office where we sat down at her conference table. A few minutes later Miss Mason and Laura came in. I noticed that the policewoman was wearing her belt with both her holstered gun and handcuffs attached to it. As Mrs. Holdstrom started to pour coffee, Miss Mason explained what was going on.

"You may remember, Andy, that Gwen told us that her husband Peter was having the hospital's accounts at Osloville Bank gone over to see if there were anything suspicious. After all, if there's something wrong at Elm Hill, covering up a theft of funds would be a good reason for it. It took a lot of laborious checking, but it appears that all the money that should have been deposited in the bank was. Also, one of their accountants came up here on the last two weekends and went over our internal accounts without finding anything obviously amiss over the last six months. Then, almost as an afterthought, they asked about the hospital's account with First National. In January, when we got our quarterly payment from the state, most of it was deposited with Osloville Bank, but $50,000 went to open an account with First National. That definitely seems strange. We've always been loyal customers of Osloville Bank, so we wouldn't normally give business to their main rival. In addition, when the next transfer of state money came in April, none of it went into the First National Account. Given the nasty competitive relationship between Osloville Bank and First National, Peter's people couldn't check with them, of course.

"As far as we can tell, Melinda Roberts, the hospital's chief bookkeeper, is the person who must have authorized the deposit. Consequently, Laura is here to question her about the deposit. She wants you, Gwen, and me to be witnesses. Laura, do you have anything to add?"

"I'll start and structure the questioning since we're investigating whether there's any evidence of criminal activity, but Gwen knows about bookkeeping and Miss Mason about the hospital, so let me know if there're specifics I'm missing." Then she gave me a mischievous smile to lighten the mood. "And Andy can scratch his nose with his thumb if he thinks I need to jiggle my handcuffs."

We then trooped deeper into the administrative suite where the bookkeeper had her office. Miss Mason tapped on the door and walked in. The room was about twelve feet square with a desk, long work table, plenty of filing cabinets, and bookshelves that were filled with files and papers. Mrs. Roberts was standing by the work table going through a tidy stack of papers. She was in her forties, fairly tall, and thin with her black hair done up in a bun. She smiled to see us even with a uniformed policewoman in the group. Certainly, she didn't appear frightened or guilty or even wary.

"Hello, Miss Mason. It's good to see you. It's always nice to have visitors and take a little break from my papers and numbers. There should be enough chairs for us if you bring them together. I know Gwen, but who else is with you?"

"Hi, Melinda. This is Andy Russell, my assistant for the summer. Also, here's Officer Laura Sanders of the Osloville Police."

Laura quickly got down to business. "Hello, Mrs. Roberts. I'm sorry to bother you, but some questions have come up, so we need to talk with you about Elm Hill. It's about Elm Hill's finances. Dr. Rydberg had an audit done of all the hospital accounts, and there seem to be some irregularities. So, I'm here to see if you can help us straighten things out."

Mrs. Roberts looked slightly surprised, but again it didn't seem to me that she was frightened or even particularly concerned.

"Of course, I'll do what I can to help. I think that I've got everything up to date."

"Okay. Mrs. Roberts, how do you pay the hospital's bills?"

"That's an easy question to answer. I get an invoice and then authorize payment through a check drawn on one of our accounts in the Osloville Bank. I do keep records pretty well, so you should be able to check the invoices against the payments easily."

"What about your account with First National Bank?"

When I heard the question, I expected her to jump, but she remained at ease.

"Oh, I set that up in January. I was a little surprised because we've always done all of our banking with Osloville and been very satisfied with them. However, a new vendor wanted to work through First National. I put $50,000 in the account in January. Then when we got the bank statement in February, I saw that the money had been transferred out."

"Where did it go? Who transferred it? Think before you answer. This is very important."

"I don't know where it went ma'am. Honestly, I don't. Dr. Rydberg or maybe Dr. Carson must have done it. The account was set up so Dr. Rydberg or I could manage it. Maybe he gave Dr. Carson access, too, since he's the Associate Director of the hospital."

Despite the changing tone of the interrogation, Mrs. Roberts didn't look concerned, but Laura's next statement changed that immediately.

"I'm sorry, Melinda, but I'm pretty sure you're a liar and a thief. Dr. Rydberg doesn't know anything about the account. Now, are you going to tell us the truth? There are three witnesses here who have no reason to lie about you."

"Please, ma'am. Please believe me. I'm not a thief. Look at our bank account. Look at our house. Look at my clothes. What could I have done with that much money? I don't know who took money out of that account, but it was Dr. Rydberg who ordered me to set it up."

"Are you calling Dr. Rydberg a liar and an embezzler?"

"No, of course not. He's a good man. He's been very good to me."

Laura stood up with a serious look on her face and unhooked the handcuffs that were attached to her belt. "Melinda Roberts, I'm arresting you on suspicion of grand theft and embezzlement. Before I take you into custody, Miss Mason has asked that I investigate something else. Please remove your blouse."

Mrs. Roberts was crying now. If anything, the request to show the upper part of her body intensified her grief and shame. Without a word, she stood up, took off her blouse, hung it on the chair behind her, and turned around slowly in a circle. It was immediately clear why Miss Mason had wanted her to disrobe. There were large bruises on her back and upper arms. She put her blouse back on, held out her arms in front of her for the handcuffs, and collapsed back on her chair once she was secured. Almost immediately, Gwen went to her side, hugged her, and gave her a handkerchief.

Laura then continued in a softer and more sympathetic voice, "Does he beat little Billy, too? Did you steal for him?"

"Please ma'am, protect Billy. He's a monster."

"Where's Billy now?"

"He's in school. Then he goes to my sister's until I finish work. What will become of him now? Can you keep him away from that brute?"

"Don't worry about that. I'll have him picked up from school. I'll personally make sure that your husband can never abuse him again."

"Thank you, ma'am. Please, though, let me tell you about the account. I don't know about who took the money out of it, but Dr. Rydberg did authorize it. Please, ma'am. Just ask him."

"What did he do? Did he tell you? Were there any witnesses?"

"No, ma'am, it was a written request. Dr. Rydberg gave it to my husband to bring to me. He's an attendant here."

"Why didn't you keep it? That's a lot of money."

"I do have it, ma'am. It's with the account information. I'd never throw away documentation. May I get it? Oh, I'm so clumsy in these handcuffs. Andy, could you please reach up and get that green folder for me? Thank you so much."

I got the folder from the top shelf of one of her bookcases, and she pulled out a slim file and opened it.

Miss Mason told her to wait a minute, went out of the room, and returned with a pair of black rubber gloves which she gave to Laura.

"Here, Officer, use my gloves. If you have to handle evidence, you won't get more fingerprints on it."

"Thank you, Miss Mason. That's a very good idea. What do you want me to look at, Melinda?"

Mrs. Roberts was certainly awkward with her hands chained, but she was able to flip through a couple of documents and point at another one. Laura lifted it by the corners with her gloved fingers and examined it closely.

"It is a directive to open an account of $50,000 in the First National Bank using some of the funds from the January state allotment. Miss Mason, could you look at this closely. Is that Dr. Rydberg's signature?"

"Please hold it up so I can get a good look at it. It certainly might be the way he signs memos, but, wait, it could be slightly off. Doctors are so illegible. Let me get Denise Nuxhall. She should be the best expert on Dr. Rydberg's signature and initials."

We waited in silence for a couple of minutes until Miss Mason returned with Mrs. Nuxhall. Both were wearing white dress gloves. Laura handed Miss Mason the paper, and she and Mrs. Nuxhall took turns to examine it closely.

"Hello, Officer Sanders. I'm Denise Nuxhall, the head secretary for Dr. Rydberg. I can't be totally certain, but I might question the authenticity. If I just glanced at it quickly, it would look okay, but when I study it, it seems slightly different from what I'm used to. I'm sorry, but that's the best that I can do. I wish I could be more definitive. I've got lots of examples of both his signature and initials. Would you like to compare them?"

"Thank you, Denise. I know that's the best you can do. I'm not an expert on handwriting. Really, I don't think that we have one here in

Osloville. We'll probably have to send it down to State Capital if we decide to do a handwriting analysis."

"Well, ma'am. There is one thing that I can tell you. I certainly didn't type the instructions. Indeed, they weren't done on either of the typewriters in our office. See the 'c' and the 'f'? There're slight chips in the keys. Both Carla and I have typewriters that don't have those imperfections."

"Denise, that's very smart. I never would have spotted that."

"Thank you for the compliment. When you're a secretary, you notice some things about your job."

"There's another thing that we haven't mentioned yet, fingerprints. We'll need to find out whose fingerprints are on the memo to Melinda. I've got a fingerprint kit in my car. Miss Mason, could you and Andy please stay here with Melinda until I'm finished?"

Once the others had left, Miss Mason walked over to Melinda and patted her reassuringly on her shoulders.

"Melinda, if you're innocent, this may work out all right. Thank heaven that you saved that memo. Whatever happens about the embezzlement, I'll make sure that Carl never hurts you or Billy again."

"Oh, thank you, ma'am."

We didn't say much more for the next few minutes until the policewoman arrived to take poor Melinda to jail.

"Thanks for your help, Miss Mason. This turned out to be far more complex than I anticipated. I've called Detective Perkins. With a theft this big, we certainly need a detective to lead the investigation. I took the fingerprints of Dr. Rydberg and his two secretaries. The other girl besides Denise almost cried when I did her. Dr. Rydberg has ordered that samples be taken from all the other typewriters in the hospital. Hopefully, something else will turn up."

After Laura left with Melinda, Miss Mason asked me to come by her office about 4:30 in case anything else came up. Since I didn't have anything else to do, I went up to Ward 2 where Mrs. Ward was very happy to learn that I still had time to read to her for several hours. When I went into the administrative suite on my way back to Miss Mason's office, Carla Fischer, who worked with Mrs. Nuxhall, was there. She was usually pretty shy, but now she was talkative from the events earlier in the afternoon.

"Oh, Andy. That policewoman fingerprinted Denise and me at our desks while you were back with Miss Mason. Denise didn't mind, but I felt scared and humiliated. Officer Sanders grabbed my wrist and fingers so tightly. I felt like I was in police custody. And then we saw poor Melinda come out in a pair of handcuffs. Now, though, it seems a little exciting. I wonder what my boyfriend will think.

"Also, Denise has been out, taking samples from the typewriters around the hospital. She thinks that she found the one they're looking for. It was in a storeroom next to the doctors' lounge. She's there now with the policewoman and several other people from the Police Department. I don't know what they're doing."

When I went on to Mrs. Holdstrom's office, she took me into Miss Mason who was waiting for us with coffee and cookies.

"We've had quite a day, and it's far from over. Several things have happened in the last couple of hours. Detective Perkins has taken over the investigation. Right now he's here with Laura, Matt Kempton, and Phil Dutton, the Police Department's fingerprint examiner. After she spotted the typewriter flaws on the memo authorizing a new account at First National Bank, Denise set about testing all the typewriters at Elm Hill. Evidently, the f and the c are very distinctive on the memo, so all she had to do was type a few letters on each machine. After an hour or so, she found an old typewriter that fit the bill in the storeroom off the doctors' lounge. She called police headquarters. They're here looking at the typewriter and taking fingerprints. Also, Phil Dutton did check the fingerprints on the memo. There were three sets. One, of course, belonged to Melinda. The other two, however, clearly weren't those of Dr. Rydberg and his secretaries, which is very good news as far as the hospital is concerned. Richard is also getting a judge to sign a warrant giving him access to First National's records about the account, so within the next day or so we should know a lot more."

"What do you think about Melinda, ma'am? I've worked with her for almost ten years. She's always seemed devoted to Dr. Rydberg and the hospital. Do you think she might be covering up for him?"

"I think she's probably completely innocent. She probably was manipulated by her husband who, according to Clem, is both nasty and lazy, but he's not smart enough to do something like this on his own. I don't think Dr. Rydberg's involved, even though Melinda might be in love with him. He's the one who asked Peter to go over our accounts, after all, which is the only reason why the theft came out. What does Peter think?"

"According to him, the new account might have got lost in the shuffle, but as soon as anyone asked what it was used for the fraud would have been exposed. From that perspective, both Dr. Rydberg and Melinda would have known that it was foolhardy to try a stunt like that."

Chapter 16 ~ An Arrest

A few minutes later Laura came by. "Phil is great. There're fingerprints in the storage room and the doctors' lounge that match one of the sets on the memo. We're indebted to Denise, too. If she hadn't caught the problems with the typeface, we never would have paid any attention to typewriters. Now we know that somebody who's been in the doctors' lounge after it was cleaned last Thursday was probably involved with forging the memo."

"What about searching Melinda's house?"

"We've got a warrant. Actually, we're about ready to leave for there. Phil is coming to check the fingerprints of that vicious husband of hers. I hope they match the final set on the memo. Richard said that you need to come but that I shouldn't ask why. You can follow us."

"Well, Laura, let's hope you're in for a good surprise. Andy, do you want to come? Gwen, I know you have to go home to your family, but I'll call you tonight if anything exciting happens."

Miss Mason drove around to the front parking lot where Detectives Perkins and Kempton, Laura, and a slight semi-bald man were standing by their unmarked police car. We followed them on a twenty-minute drive to a small bungalow with an untidy front yard. There were two police cars waiting in front of it when we arrived. When they saw Detective Perkins, two beefy uniformed cops got out of one the cars. Much to my surprise, a jail matron got out of the other and removed Melinda from the cage in its back. The prisoner was wearing a black-and-white striped prison dress, had her handcuffs attached to a tight chain around her waist, and held her head down in shame. Detective Perkins pounded on the door as the rest of us straggled up the walk behind him. Since Carl Roberts worked the eleven to seven shift, he was presumably asleep. It wasn't surprising that it was several minutes before he opened the door, bleary eyed and wearing a white undershirt and tattered blue jeans. He was immediately hostile and aggressive.

"What the hell do you want?" When he saw his shackled wife, though, his mood changed instantly. "Got the bitch, did you? That's great. What's that high and mighty Dr. Rydberg going to think now that his little pet got caught stealing from him?"

Detective Perkins ignored both extremes of emotion and just gave him a formal notification. "Mr. Roberts, your wife has been arrested for embezzlement. We have a search warrant for your house which we will execute now with or without your cooperation. Do you understand?"

"Sure, I don't have any objection, especially since you've got that stupid cow chained up. How many of the neighbors do you think are watching you through their curtains, missy? They're going to be mocking you until kingdom come."

Once we were all inside, Detective Perkins continued, "Your wife claims that you brought her the document authorizing the bank transaction that constitutes the theft. What do you say to that?"

"She's a liar and a bitch. Always was and always will be. She's trying to save her own worthless skin. Don't believe her. This is an honest workingman's neighborhood. She always thought she was better than us. There're lots of folks around here that will laugh now she's headed to state prison."

"Well, that should be easy enough to prove. There are three sets of fingerprints on that memo. If none of them are yours, you're obviously in the clear. Officer Sanders is very capable of taking prints and brought her kit with her. Laura, would you please help Mr. Roberts clear his name?"

This last bit of sarcasm enraged the man, but each of the patrolmen grabbed one of his arms so he was helpless. Laura printed him on the coffee table and handed her card to the man I assumed was Phil Dutton. He pulled out a magnifying glass and studied the prints and then held the glass over something in a file that he laid out on the coffee table. He looked up, smiled, and said he was almost certain there was a match. Laura unhooked the cuffs from her belt while the two policemen twisted Roberts' arms behind him for her. After she had secured his hands behind his back, the policemen forced him down on the couch in the room. Miss Mason then approached the prisoner and pulled a white rubber gag from her voluminous handbag.

"You don't have to be a psychiatric nurse to see how distraught he is. Do you want to use this to save us listening to his screaming and swearing while you search the house?"

"We'll open his mouth, if you'll put it in, ma'am."

Once Roberts was attended to, the matron, Miss Mason, and I stayed in the living room with the two prisoners while the others spread out to search the house. After a few minutes, Miss Mason briefly left the house and returned with a green duffle bag. In about half an hour, we heard a triumphant yell from the attic. Detective Perkins soon emerged carrying a black briefcase by the corners in gloved hands. He put it down gently on the coffee table and waited for the others to gather around. He said that he had found it in a space under some floor boards in the partially completed attic. When he tried to open the case, it was locked. The older of the two policemen asked Carl and Melinda whether the briefcase belonged to either of them. They both shook their heads no. He said if that's true, they couldn't object to opening it. He pulled out a large penknife, and sprung the lock, revealing that the case was half filled with twenty dollar bills. After a couple of comments from the onlookers, Detective Perkins took charge.

"Carl Roberts, there's enough evidence now to arrest you on suspicion of grand theft. We'll have to wait to see whether your fingerprints are on the case or the money, of course, but there's plenty of reason to hold you now. Oh, Miss Mason. Do you have something to say?"

"Yes. Mr. Roberts, substantial bruises were found upon the body of your wife upon her arrest and upon the body of your son when the police picked him up from school. Both testified that you regularly beat them. Clearly, you are mentally ill and need to be confined to a psychiatric hospital."

She then rose and approached him holding a thin file which she had presumably taken from the duffle bag. "Here, as you can see, is an order signed by Judge Welch and Dr. Carson committing you to the Downsville Asylum. If they ever can cure you, you'll have to come back here, of course, to face charges of theft and assault and battery on your wife and son."

Roberts tried, unsuccessfully, to scream through his gag and briefly thrust his body up and down and kicked his legs until the two uniformed officers pinned him down. The short struggle made me see another function of gagging a prisoner or patient. If they became violent, they'd become breathless pretty quickly. As Roberts sagged back, Laura walked up to the couch, stood over him, and said sweetly.

"You are violent and criminally insane, aren't you? We'll need to get you bundled up so you can't cause any more problems until your transported to Downsville, won't we? You really need it to keep you safe. John, Bill, please get him on his feet and get his arms ready."

She turned and took a white strait jacket from Miss Mason, held up the sleeves, pulled first the right and then the left of Roberts' arms into them once he'd been freed of his handcuffs, and with a sweet smile told him, "We'll have someone special buckle you up."

She stepped aside, as the matron brought Melinda face-to-face with her husband, whose eyes bulged in hatred, and unlocked her handcuffs. Laura then turned Carl around so his back was toward the women.

"Here, Melinda. You've got four straps across the back and sleeves from the front that need to be buckled together at the back. If you have questions, Miss Mason can help you."

Melinda didn't need any help, and she was actually smiling when her handcuffs were reattached.

Chapter 17 ~ The Disappearing Doc

The next morning, I got a call asking me to go to Miss Mason's office rather than Ward 2 when I finished on the Violent Ward. When I got there, she and Mrs. Holdstrom were enjoying coffee and strudel.

"Hi, Andy. Relax for a few minutes and help yourself to the refreshments. We have a two o'clock appointment. Gwen and I have some news for you as well.

"The Police Department has been putting a lot of effort into fingerprint analysis since last evening. One thing came out nicely. The briefcase that Richard found at the Roberts house had Carl's fingerprints on it but not Melinda's. Another thing turned a little messy, though. With all the excitement about the Roberts yesterday, there wasn't any time to follow up on the fingerprints in the doctors' lounge. This morning, Laura got a brainstorm. She and Phil Dutton came back and printed the doctors' coffee mugs as a shortcut to discovering whose prints were on the memo that Carl took to Melinda. They found lots of the prints that they were looking for on the coffee mug of Dr. Max Matthews, one of the permanent staff members. Unfortunately, there must have been lots of gossip about the police going through the lounge and the storeroom yesterday. Dr. Matthews didn't come to work today. When we called his home, his wife said he didn't come home from work yesterday. It looks like he may have got the wind up and flown the coop. Laura is going to interview her this afternoon and asked me to come along since I know so much about the hospital. Gwen needs to stay here to handle several of my appointments that can't be delayed. I want you to come with me to take notes."

Mrs. Holdstrom helpfully interjected and asked whether I would like to use a stenographer's book or a notepad. When I admitted to a total ignorance of shorthand, she gave me a legal pad and two pens, one blue and one red. A little after 1:30, Laura tapped on the door. As we approached her patrol car from the back, I started to walk toward her side of the car, but she took my arm and steered me in the other direction.

"Sorry, Andy. My fingerprint kit and some other stuff are in the back. You'll have to sit in the cage for this trip. You don't mind, do you?"

"Well, I do feel a little nervous."

"Don't be silly. Miss Mason is here, I'm not going to cart you off to jail like Melinda. Here, let me open the door and get you settled down on the seat. See, there's nothing to it. By the way, are you disappointed I didn't have to fingerprint you? Or, would you have felt humiliated like that one secretary?"

"I might have been a little humiliated. I do have a question for you if you don't think it's impertinent. Why do you like to think of yourself as Nancy Drew?"

"I'm complimented that you pay attention to me. In my job you see lots of bad things that can make you look down on civilians. I know you thought Matt is cynical and harsh when he plays *bad cop*. Nancy is innocent and likes to help people. Now that you mention it, I think that that's the way I'd like to feel more often."

As we drove off, Laura told Miss Mason that the ambulance from the state hospital had come for Roberts a little before noon. Both of them appeared satisfied that he would be in Downsville's equivalent of our Violent Ward within a couple of hours. Miss Mason also complimented her on how quickly her investigation had produced results.

"Thank you, ma'am. This is what I find exciting about police work. Mostly, it's pretty routine, boring, frustrating and sometimes frightening. Still, something like this makes you so proud of accomplishing something. But I can't take much credit, almost every big step was taken by somebody else. For example, without Denise's applying her knowledge of typewriters or Phil's skill with fingerprints, we wouldn't have gotten very far. I guess that that's another thing that police work teaches you, you can't get very far unless different people apply their special skills."

"You're very wise, Laura. Maybe that's why our Black Angels will succeed in the end. We've got a variety of people with very different talents and skills. By the way, what's happened to Billy Roberts?"

"I didn't want the shrews from Social Services to get their claws into him. Also, I'm pretty sure that Melinda should be released in a day or two since it looks like she was just an innocent dupe of her husband and this disappearing doctor. I picked him up from school and took him to my sister's. Karen is a housewife who has the time to be nice to him. Please don't spread the word around."

"I think you did the right thing. I hope that he's quickly reunited with his mom. He must be feeling scared and alone."

When we pulled into the driveway of a very nice two-story brick house, Mrs. Matthews, who must have been watching for us, opened the front door and came out to greet us. She was a tall blonde, still beautiful in her late forties, and wearing expensive clothes and a very forlorn expression.

"Please come in. I'll try to be helpful. Why are you looking for Max? Why is there a policewoman?"

While Laura was the official investigator, Miss Mason seemed to take charge.

"Hello, Mrs. Matthews. We're sorry to bother you, but your husband seems to be missing. We're very concerned, so we contacted the police to help us. I'm Carol Mason, the Director of Nursing at Elm Hill. We've met a few times at hospital functions. This is Officer Laura Sanders from the Osloville Police, and this is my assistant, Andy Russell."

"Thank you, Miss Mason. I do remember seeing you. Let's sit in the living room. I've got some refreshments prepared. I'll be back in a minute."

When she and her housekeeper returned and we were all comfortably seated, Miss Mason took the lead. "I'm truly sorry to bring you very distressing news, Mrs. Matthews, but I don't think that there's any way to sugarcoat it. In the last week we've found evidence that a large amount of money, $50,000, was embezzled from the hospital. Yesterday, during the investigation, Officer Sanders and the police turned up some evidence that your husband may have been involved. They didn't realize that the evidence pointed toward him until this morning, but people in the hospital must have seen what they were doing yesterday. In any event, nobody's seen him since he left the hospital at 5:00. Are you sure that he didn't come home last night?"

"No, he didn't. The kids and I had to eat supper alone."

Here, Laura took over the questioning. "Weren't you worried, ma'am? I don't think that you contacted the police."

Mrs. Matthews sobbed for a moment and then got control of herself. "I thought he was out with his hussy again. Sometimes he doesn't come home. For the last five years he's turned to younger women. The stupid nurses fall all over themselves when a doctor crooks his finger at them."

"I'm so sorry for you, ma'am. Doctors should know better, but one thing I've learned as a policewoman is that even seemingly good people can do bad things. Do you have any idea where he could have gone?"

"Yes, Officer, I might. Last year I had a private detective follow him. He found out that he was having an affair with a red-headed witch of a nurse from the Medical Center and that they were using an apartment he'd rented for their trysts. I have the address imprinted on my brain, Apartment 203 at 756 Conover Street. I made him end the affair, but he may have kept the apartment. I know he's taken up with another tramp from the evenings he's spent away from home these last few months."

"Ma'am, may I use your telephone? We need to get someone there right away."

"Certainly, there's an extension by the bookcase over there."

Laura walked over to the telephone and asked the operator to connect her to police headquarters. "Hello, Richard? Glad I caught you. Mrs. Matthews says that he's had mistresses and used Apartment 203 at 756 Conover Street. You need to check whether he's still got the apartment. Okay, I'll ask her."

"Ma'am, will you let our detectives search this house. Or, do they need to get a search warrant."

"They certainly have my blessings. I hope they catch the creep and throw him in jail for a good long time!"

While Laura went through the doctor's office and I tried to stay inconspicuous, Miss Mason comforted Mrs. Matthews. The poor woman was heartbroken on one level but also seemed to realize that this might free her from the long depressing nightmare created by her unfaithful husband. Her family back East was wealthy, so she didn't have financial worries. When Laura came back in about twenty minutes, she said she hadn't found anything that was obviously useful but that she was sure that the detectives would want to search the house later.

Miss Mason hugged Mrs. Matthews and told her to call Dr. Rydberg if she needed any help.

Laura decided that she'd drop us off at Elm Hill and then go to the apartment on Conover to see if anything had turned up there. Once we were in the car, Miss Mason raised another possibility.

"Laura, I've got a bad feeling if Matthews did move on to a new mistress. Some nurses suspect that Andy's friend, Carly Henderson, started having a secret affair about Christmas time. Unfortunately, that fits the time frame. She came to us from a Catholic high school where the nuns are very strict. I'm pretty sure that she would be quite naïve about sex and could have fallen under a doctor's blandishments quite easily. She's sweet and she's cute, so she would make an attractive target."

When we got back to Elm Hill, Laura parked in front of Brackman, let me out of the back seat, and transferred her gun and handcuffs from her purse to her belt. She and Miss Mason then went into the dormitory since it was over an hour after Carly's shift had ended. I waited on the front porch, hoping for a happy ending. When they came out in less than ten minutes, they were alone and Miss Mason was looking grim.

"She hadn't come back from the hospital after her shift, but Laura found some very expensive jewelry hidden under her mattress that she certainly couldn't have purchased herself. We're going to search for her in the hospital. She was in the Violent Ward this morning, wasn't she?"

"Yes, she was. We were so busy that I can't be absolutely sure, but I think that she looked a little upset."

The two women drove off toward the hospital to look for her there, while I went around the back of Brackman to go to my room. As soon as I came to the stairs going down to the basement, I saw a forlorn figure in a white pinafore sitting at the bottom. When I reached her, she looked up with a devastated expression on her face.

"Oh, Andy. I can see that you know."

"Carly, I'm so sorry. Are you going to run away?"

"There's nowhere I can go. Please stay with me for a few minutes. You may be my only friend. He left me last night and told me that I was a little fool. The other nurses despise me for being naughty with a doctor. Please, just hold me for a minute." We embraced and then headed silently back up the stairs toward the hospital. When we reached Mrs. Holdstrom's office, she looked at us sadly, took us to the conference table in Miss Mason's office, and said that she'd get Miss Mason and Officer Sanders. Laura got there first and immediately placed Carly under arrest, but she waited for Miss Mason before taking her away. When Miss Mason arrived a few minutes later, she went to Carly and hugged her.

"Carly, I'm so sorry for you. I think you've been the victim of a wicked man, but the police have to arrest you. Officer Sanders has agreed that I can talk to you for a few minutes. First, what the police are interested in are the embezzlement and where the creep is now. Don't say anything about the first until you meet with one of the hospital lawyers tomorrow morning because that's what you can be jailed for, but anything you can do to help catch him can only benefit you. Do you understand?"

"Yes ma'am, but I can't help. We met about seven at his apartment like we'd arranged. We made love, but he was very rough and domineering. Afterwards he said that the police were after him, so he had to go away. I asked him if I could go with him, but he said I had to look after myself."

"Did he take anything with him from the apartment?"

"I don't know. I didn't see him take anything, but he was at the apartment when I got there so he could have loaded stuff in his car before I arrived."

"When did your affair start?"

"Last November. He had two patients on the Violent Ward at that time. One of them was mine and we started talking about her. He told me that I was smart and beautiful and that his wife didn't appreciate him anymore."

"Did he have other close friends or contacts on the Violent Ward?"

"I don't think so. He said that Miss Mason didn't give doctors enough respect. He didn't seem to like anyone else. I think Amy was jealous because the ward's *little dope* had snared a doctor."

"Did he have anything to do with Carrie or Jenny?"

"No, they weren't his patients. He never even talked about Jenny. He gossiped a little bit about Carrie, but so did everybody else. He didn't seem interested in her treatment."

After Laura escorted Carly to her squad car, Mrs. Holdstrom came in for a wrap-up. Miss Mason said Dr. Rydberg had agreed to provide a lawyer for Carly. She probably was an accomplice, but Matthews and Roberts were the people who were responsible. I said that this didn't seem to be related to the Adams murder. Instead, we seemed to be getting new problems without making any progress on Carrie.

"You're right and you're wrong, Andy. I very much doubt that Matthews and his embezzlement have any connection with Judge Adams and Carrie, but they do give us a major clue that we hadn't thought of before. Did you ever read *The Purloined Letter* by Edgar Allan Poe?"

"Yes, I read it in high school, but I don't see the relevance."

"Sometimes you need to look for what's simple, not complex. The answer can be hidden in plain sight."

Then she told us, and we laughed at what we hadn't seen.

Chapter 18 ~ Suspicion of a New Aide

Presumably because of Carly's arrest, I got a note from Miss Rayburn at supper telling me that the day shift in the Violent Ward should report at 6:30 instead of 7:00 for a special organization meeting. When we assembled there was a student nurse who was wearing a black rubber apron over her uniform. Miss Rayburn introduced her as Helga Gerlach from Ward 2, whom she had selected to replace Carly because of her reputation for being kind and caring to her senile dementia patients. She was outgoing and cheery and was a six-foot statuesque blonde of about twenty. Miss Rayburn then turned her attention to me.

"Andy, you'll take over Miss Delaware and Mrs. Quick from Carly's patients to replace Mrs. Strickland and Miss Peters. Also, thank you, Amy, for helping get Helga oriented. Finally, Mrs. Greene and I are going to visit each patient in their room to tell them about Carly. Once we get started, you can follow us around with your normal procedures. There'll obviously be a significant delay in our morning routine. For example, breakfast will be at least half an hour later than normal, but I'm hoping that a full explanation and a little hand holding can reduce the reaction to such momentous news. If you see someone starting to get agitated, please inform Mrs. Greene or Miss Rice immediately. We can delay lunch so we can have two hour-and-a-half sessions of hydrotherapy."

The morning was more chaotic than Mrs. Rayburn had feared, showing me firsthand the contagious effect of patients' losing control of themselves. By late morning, out of our nineteen patients, three had been packed, seven given hydrotherapy, and three confined to their cells in strait jackets by Amy and Thomas.

It was almost an hour late when we sat down to lunch. Helga asked to sit with me and proved a cheery companion. She was familiar with most of her new duties, except some of the restraints. I offered to show her how to use the iron anklets and restraining belts after lunch and referred her to Big Bertha for instruction in straitjacketing. Finally, we chatted and laughed about working in small town drugstores and left the table giggling about how some patients tried to fool pharmacists.

After lunch we turned to our nurse's notes which, due to the chaos on the ward, took longer than normal, so that it was two o'clock by the time we finished.

I then showed her where two restraining belts were kept out of sight at the nurses' station and how the belt and the wrist cuffs that were attached to it worked with their small metal posts that were locked into a tab that came over the belt or the cuff. She asked me to serve as a dummy and quickly had the belt securely fitted and my wrists locked into padded cuffs that were surprisingly comfortable. As she briefly admired her handiwork, I got quite a shock when I heard Laura Sanders' familiar voice, "Excuse me, Miss, but I need your patient. I'm questioning the staff here about Carly Henderson. Who are you?"

The sight of the uniformed policewoman flustered Helga who blushed deeply and fumbled with the keys as she tried to unlock the belt and cuffs. "I'm Helga Gerlach, the new nursing student who's replacing Carly. I'm coming from Ward 2 for patients with senile dementia and haven't used a restraining belt before. Andy showed me how to put one on a patient. Now, I'm practicing on him."

Helga finally got me out of the belt, but she didn't seem to have allayed all of Laura's suspicion.

"How did you get selected on such short notice?"

"My nurse manager recommended me to Miss Rayburn, the manager of this Ward, because of the very good rapport that I've developed with the dementia patients on Ward 2. She felt that maybe I could have a calming influence on the agitated patients down here. Mrs. Lawrence asked me if I'd be interested in moving to the Violent Ward and, when I agreed, recommended me."

"Why are you wearing a rubber apron? Were you afraid that Andy was going to do something nasty on you?"

I saw a look of panic flit across Helga's face at these questions, but she answered calmly enough. "No ma'am, of course not. This morning a patient soiled my uniform with her bedpan, even though I was wearing my apron. This is the only spare one that I have here today, so I want to do everything I could to protect it."

"Well, do you mind coming along with us for a couple of minutes to see if you can help?"

"Certainly, ma'am. I'm happy to cooperate."

We followed Laura into the Nurse Manager's suite and sat around the conference table in the side office. She turned first to Helga.

"Since this is your first day here, you obviously haven't worked with Carly. Still, is there anything that you can tell me about her?"

"Yes, ma'am. I live in the nurses' dormitory with her. Everyone believed that she was having an affair. It's very hard to hide an affair among the girls and people started treating her with suspicion which made her withdraw. Nobody had any idea that she was stealing from the hospital. Last night there was wild gossip about her, but I don't think that it had much basis in fact."

"Thank you, Helga. That's about what everyone has told me."

"Yes, ma'am. Can I leave now?"

"That's fine, Helga. Thanks for being cooperative.

"Andy, what do you know about Carly?"

"Not much more than Helga. Once I got to know her, she was very helpful. Yesterday, I found her sitting by the basement door into my room. She was despondent and resigned, but I don't know anything about what she did with Dr. Matthews."

"I don't think anyone here did. Come on, I've brought some things for Gwen and Miss Mason that you should find interesting."

We didn't say anything until we were out of the Violent Ward. Then Laura started to tease me, but she quickly turned serious. "Andy, should I feel insulted? You seem scared of me, but you let that big blonde truss you up in leathers."

"Well, you're a policewoman. She's just a nursing student so there shouldn't be anything to be afraid of. She certainly can't arrest people or have them committed here."

"What do you know about her?"

"Not much more than what she said to you. She told us this morning that she grew up in Swedesboro, worked in a drug store for a year after high school, and came to Elm Hill for nursing school last fall because her mother knew one of the nurses here. This morning was very chaotic because the patients got upset over Carly. She worked very well with them and was very cooperative with our staff. She's nice, and I like her."

"Well, don't like her too much."

"You seem pretty suspicious of her."

"There was something about her that didn't strike me as quite right. I'll talk to her Nurse Manager from Ward 2 later to see if there's something concrete."

We had reached the top of the stairs when we were interrupted by Christine Maxwell, the charge nurse from Ward 2 who was just coming off duty. "Hi, Andy. I see you're wearing your nurse's cap outside the Violent Ward. Is this the first time?"

"Oh. Hi, Mrs. Maxwell. I just forgot to take it off and put it in my locker."

"Well, don't be embarrassed. The girls will probably like you better for it. By the way, thank you so much for working with Mrs. Ward. You've really perked her up."

"That's nice to know. I like her. I'm sorry that I've been so busy this week that I haven't been able to keep to our schedule."

"Oh, that's all right. She understands. Actually, she's very excited about your graduation this weekend."

Chapter 19 ~ Tracking the Suspect

I felt a little sensitive about my cap. There didn't appear to be anything that I could do with it, so I kept it on as we walked the rest of the way to Miss Mason's office. When we got there, Miss Mason pointed us to the conference table, called Mrs. Holdstrom to get refreshments, and said that she was glad that I was starting to wear my cap outside the Violent Ward. Laura patted me on the arm and gave what she thought was a comforting explanation. "He left his cap on because he was distracted by the chaos of the ward today. He's a little ashamed to be seen in it. Really, Andy, it's not very feminine.

"Come to think of it, maybe wearing it does honor the nurses who, from what I've see, do a great job in caring for the patients here."

This response drew a smile and nod from Miss Mason as we moved on to the business at hand. Laura pulled a tape from her purse as the rest of us began to enjoy our coffee and cookies.

"We have an interrogation that Richard wants you to hear. It's my interview with Dr. Matthews' mistress last night. I'm proud of what happened. I didn't even try to intimidate her and kept my handcuffs in my purse. Instead, I reassured a frightened woman and struck a goldmine.

"After I transported Carly to jail, I called the Medical Center and asked about Wendy Carter's schedule. They said she was working the evening shift on the third floor surgical ward so I went to the hospital right away. I found the charge nurse at the nurses' station who said that Wendy was administering medications and asked me to wait half an hour until she was finished so her rounds wouldn't be disrupted. I agreed and waited in a small conference room behind the nurses' station. The charge nurse brought her in when she became available, but when she saw my uniform she became obviously frightened. Let me play a recording of the interview for you."

Laura clicked on the tape player and after a brief buzz of static, "Thank you so much, Mrs. Sturgis. Could you please close the door?

"What's the matter Miss Carter? You look scared. There's nothing to be frightened about. I just have to ask you some questions. Here, let me take you to a chair."

"Please, ma'am. Is she having me arrested? I haven't even talked to him for over six months. I've heard such bad stories about how the matrons treat nurses in the county jail."

"Please calm down, Wendy. You can't be put in jail for having an affair. Also, I think the matrons are scared about mistreating nurses now. Are you talking about an affair with Dr. Matthews? Did his wife threaten you? Please tell me what happened. You won't get in trouble for it. I promise."

"Yes, ma'am. I'm so ashamed. It started at a hospital Christmas party. He came without his wife for some reason. He's very attractive and a doctor, so I was quite flattered when he started flirting with me. He offered to drive me home, and I asked him in for coffee. He started stroking me, and I tensed up a little. Then he apologized and said that his wife was frigid. Somehow that made me want him. After that, we made love about once a week, mostly in an apartment that he rented on Conover Street. Then in November, his wife found out about us. I don't know how. Perhaps someone saw us together."

"Did she threaten to have you arrested?

Here, the nurse started to cry. "No, she didn't talk about the police, but I couldn't think of anything else when I saw you in your uniform. She came to my apartment the week before Thanksgiving. She told me who she was and ordered me to go to my living room and sit down. She's quite attractive but a lot older than I am. She said that I had seduced her husband and that she would not permit me to continue our relationship. I started to cry. I should have just apologized, but I retorted that it wouldn't have happened if she had been willing to love him. This enraged her. I thought she might hit me. Instead, she said with real venom, 'You're an unscrupulous slut, aren't you? Are you a little liar or a little fool? For your information, he's the one who doesn't want me. I'm the one with the money, so he'll do what I tell him. In addition, I'm a good friend with the Hospital Director, so if you ever try to sneak around again, I'll have your nursing career destroyed.'"

"Well, Wendy. There's a huge scandal. Soon after he broke off with you, Dr. Matthews seduced a nursing student at Elm Hill Psychiatric Hospital. Then he evidently embezzled $50,000. The aide and two other possible accomplices were arrested earlier today. Matthews escaped yesterday with most of the money. Please be honest, Wendy. Do you know anything about this?"

"Oh no, ma'am. I had an affair with him, but we never talked about any crime. Please believe me. I haven't even spoken to him since his wife threatened me."

"I believe you. Since you haven't run off with him, you don't look guilty. Then again, he left his other mistress behind. The embezzlement occurred in January. Now think carefully, did he say anything that might have indicated that he was planning to steal from Elm Hill?"

"No. If his wife does control his money, maybe that's why he wanted to steal."

"That's a good possibility. Now, think again, do you have any idea where he might be hiding? I know you may still love him, but the sooner he's caught, the better it will be for everyone."

"Oh, ma'am. I wouldn't help or hide him. He's so wicked. To steal and to seduce another poor girl, it's so awful. Do you think he's here in town? I can give you the address where his secret apartment is."

"We got that from his wife yesterday. His new mistress met him there last night and told us that he was packing his car to escape."

"Well, in that case, I do have an idea. We spent four days in State Capital when he went to a medical convention. It might have been the best time I ever had with him because we had so much time together. We stayed in the Westview Apartments on Laurel Street where he shared a place with some local doctors. The apartment was on the third floor, number #306 … I'm pretty sure. I hope that helps."

"Thank you so much, Wendy. Is there anything I can do for you?"

"Oh Lord, I don't think so. This is such a huge scandal that I'm sure our affair will come out pretty quickly. Then I'll be fired without a reference. Oh, why was I so stupid?"

Laura clicked off the tape and continued with a huge smile on her face. "Luckily, the charge nurse gave me a telephone and I was able to reach Richard within a couple of minutes. He called me back later with exciting news. He has a good friend, Ricky Flynn, who's a lieutenant on the State Capitol police. After talking with Richard, he went to check out the apartment within an hour. When he and three patrolmen got there, they saw lights on in the apartment. Then it got dramatic. They pounded on the door and heard a window being opened inside. One of the patrolmen kicked down the door, they rushed in and found a guy in the bedroom who turned out to be Matthews. Lt. Flynn looked out the window and saw a woman going down the fire escape with a briefcase in her hand. Fortunately, he had thought ahead and sent one of the patrolmen around to the back. As she reached the bottom of the ladder he stepped out of the shadows, grabbed her, and placed her under arrest.

"The woman was Missy Robinson, a nurse at State Capital General Hospital. She was naked under her unzipped dress. Because she hit the officer over the head with the briefcase, she was arrested for aggravated assault and resisting arrest as well as for being an accomplice to the embezzlement. The briefcase had almost $30,000. So between that and what we found at the Roberts house, Elm Hill should get most of its embezzled money back. Richard and Matt will escort the 'Disappearing Doc,' and a matron and I will put his 'Pantyless Pet' into a patrol car cage and haul her back."

"Congratulations, Laura. I didn't realize the police had such a sense of humor with their nicknames. You made Gwen and Andy giggle. Have you told Mrs. Matthews?"

"Well, I am proud. This is the biggest arrest that I've ever been involved in. I never would have believed when I went to the hospital last night that we'd have Matthews under lock and key within a couple of hours. Yes, we did notify people. Matt and I visited Mrs. Matthews this morning. She was overjoyed when we told her that her nasty hubby had been captured but shocked that he had another nurse for a mistress. She'd already seen Carly's picture in this morning's paper and couldn't believe that her husband could have been sneaking around with such a young girl. Since she's the one who has the money, I don't think that Matthews is going to get bailed out before his trial. He didn't openly abuse women, but he's betrayed four women.

"In addition to the incarceration of those two, we've got some news about the others that Matthews tried to involve in his scheme. The State's Attorney is now pretty sure that Melinda was just manipulated by Matthews and her husband. She was released at lunchtime. The news isn't as good about Carly, but at least she won't be sharing a cell with Missy the tramp in Crawford State Prison for Women. The lawyer worked out a deal with the State's Attorney where she'll plead guilty to a misdemeanor and tell us all that she knows about Matthews in return for a sentence in the county jail.

"Finally, there even may be some hope for 'Wicked Wendy,' who'll probably lose her job even though she didn't do anything criminal. In fact, from our perspective, she's a heroine since we couldn't have captured the creep without her help. I told Richard about her predicament. He felt sorry for her and called the Director of the Medical Center to plead her case. Doctor Ryerson listened patiently and then laughed, before explaining that she would easily get a job working for a doctor, probably at a significantly higher salary than her credentials would normally warrant."

I interjected, "Ma'am, I hope you don't think I'm being disrespectful, but I wondered about a couple of things from Monday. I noticed that you had got Roberts committed before we even went to their house and that you and Officer Sanders didn't just take Roberts into custody but mocked him as well."

"No, Andy. You're not being disrespectful. If you wonder about something it's good to ask. Luckily, I have the contacts to get a committal in an extreme case, which I hope you agree Roberts was. I'm a firm believer in involuntary committals for people who are seriously mentally ill, although I know that this can be abused. I'd certainly like to see more safeguards, but some people need to be institutionalized to protect both themselves and the people around them. In Roberts' case, a committal will keep him under lock and key far longer than a criminal prosecution would. I think that this is essential because he's a clear threat to Melinda and Billy. I hope that doesn't make you think worse of our field. We're not perfect, but I honestly don't see how we can be.

"I think that I can speak for Officer Sanders as well as myself about how we treated Roberts. Both of us in our professions see a considerable number of women and children who have been abused by men. It makes my blood boil to think how leniently these men are often treated by the law and the police. They seem to think it's their right to hurt women. You're right that we may have let our professionalism slip a little, but just think what he'd done. You saw the bruises that he inflicted on poor Melinda. Then he tried to blame her for his own crime. Think how humiliating it was for her to be escorted to and from her house in a prison dress and chains. In any event, he would have ended up in a strait jacket and a gag. That's how the police handle the criminally insane. If I were back at Downsville, I wouldn't be mean to him if he were one of my patients. Now that he's institutionalized, he should be cared for like the women in our Violent Ward are, with professionalism and compassion."

Laura patted my arm a little tentatively. "Andy, I hope you don't think I'm a bad person. I don't hurt my prisoners, even those who have tried to attack me. Roberts is a monster, so I didn't mind his being humiliated. I have to admit I enjoyed watching Melinda buckle up his strait jacket. Did you know that we have two padded cells for confining out-of-control mental patients?"

I smiled back at her. "I agree. It was poetic justice. You don't seem to realize how much I look up to you and Miss Mason."

"Well, in any event, it certainly turned out to be a very eventful evening. When Richard called to say that Matthews and Mistress Missy were in State Capital jail cells, I was so excited and felt almost as good as if I'd handcuffed them myself, like I'd done Roberts and Carly earlier in the day. Matt helped me celebrate later and told me that I was turning into a good detective. You know, I think that yesterday was the best day of my life, at least until our wedding."

It was my turn to pat her in congratulations. "Oh, Laura. I'm so happy for you. You should be proud."

"Well, thank you. I really am."

Chapter 20 ~ Interrogating the Aide

The next morning the patients in the Violent Ward were still upset, although it wasn't anywhere nearly as bad as Wednesday. Consequently, we spent most of our time trying to maintain calm. Helga was very good with her patients, but she seemed a little tense at times. Mrs. Holdstrom came down to see me as we were getting luncheon served, back at the regular time, thank heaven. She pulled me aside and whispered that I should go up to Ward 2 to say goodbye for the weekend to Mrs. Ward but to be sure that I was back in her office by 2:00. Mrs. Ward was in a cheery mood and told me to forget about Elm Hill for the next few days and to enjoy my family, friends, and the thrill of graduation. She said that Dr. Rydberg had agreed to have her old optometrist treat her, and she hoped that she could get new glasses that would allow her to read again. I also asked her about Helga. Her view of Helga was that she walked on water.

"Oh, Helga Gerlach is simply an angel. She was so good with her patients. She has a knack for caring and empathy that even most of the real nurses don't approach. For example, I'm pretty sure that she was the only one who could make patients feel that they were receiving therapy, not punishment, when they were being packed. When she left for the Violent Ward so suddenly yesterday, there were mixed feelings. On the one hand, most of us were shocked that she wouldn't be here to care for us anymore, but several of us got to thinking that maybe those patients need her more than we do. I think that a lot of the old ladies here love her and want what's best for her."

I kissed her goodbye on the cheek and told her that I'd see her the next Wednesday. I reached Mrs. Holdstrom's office at almost exactly the stroke of two where I found a serious-looking Miss Mason waiting for me.

"Hi, Andy. Laura is going to interrogate Helga in a few minutes. That stupid girl definitely lied to her yesterday. Laura is going to do more than jiggle her handcuffs to get the truth out of her. Let's go to our listening room."

Once we were seated in the little room, Miss Mason turned on the recorder in the conference room and must have done something that let Laura know we were ready because she whispered, "I'll signal Denise to get her."

A few moments later we heard a door open, a chair scrape back, and Laura greet the newcomers.

"Thank you so much, Denise. Let me take your arm."

The door closed again followed by Helga's frightened voice. "Oh, Officer. Are you arresting me? What have I done?"

"You're not under arrest yet, Helga, but if you did something criminal, I'll have to take you to jail. You lied to me yesterday, so we have to find out what you did. See, I have to wear my gun because you're a criminal suspect. You're a big girl, much bigger than I am, and I have to make sure you don't attack me. I'm putting a handcuff on your right wrist. Sit in this chair, and I'll cuff you to the wooden arm. There, now you're secure, and we're both protected. Do you understand?"

"Yes, ma'am. I know I'm very tall for a girl, but I've never been violent."

"Well, I think it's better that you don't have any temptation to act up. Now, do you know why you're here? Do you admit that you lied? Do you think I'm so stupid that I wouldn't check up on something suspicious? Tell me what your lie was. Then we can figure out what you are up to."

Helga had started to cry, but she complied to Laura's demands with only a little hesitation. "I know I was stupid, ma'am. Please believe me. I told you yesterday that my nurse manager, Mrs. Lawrence, asked me if I wanted to move to the Violent Ward, but in actuality I asked her to recommend me to Miss Rayburn. I'm so sorry. How did you catch me?"

"You obviously are not much of a sneak, Helga, which speaks in your favor. Carly wasn't arrested until a few minutes before 5:00 p.m. Since Mrs. Lawrence leaves for her home and her family at 5:00, it's almost impossible that she would have learned about Carly in time to talk to you. Didn't you think of that?"

"No, ma'am. I don't usually lie and sneak."

"That's what Mrs. Lawrence said. She had found you to be completely trustworthy. She could hardly believe what you did. In fact, she said that the senior staff thinks that you're the best student nurse they've ever had at Elm Hill. Now are you going to confess and tell the truth?"

"Yes, ma'am. I'm sorry I was bad. I just was scared."

"Okay, now tell me what happened."

"I was on the 3-to-11 shift on Ward 2 this week. A little before 4:30 I got called to the telephone. Miss Strong was calling me. She said that the police were investigating Carly Henderson and that she was going to be arrested. She asked if I would like to move to the Violent Ward to work with a wider variety of the mentally ill than we have on Ward 2. She said that it would be very good experience for me. I said that it sounded interesting and went to see Mrs. Lawrence before she went off duty. She was shocked that sweet Carly was in trouble with the law and said that she would support me in whatever I wanted to do because I had been so good with her patients. She called Miss Rayburn, and they agreed that I would move to the Violent Ward immediately if you took poor Carly away."

"Now you're being a good girl Helga and telling the truth."

"How do you know, ma'am?"

"Amy Strong called you from Brackman Hall. The operators at Elm Hill love to eavesdrop and gossip. Certainly, saying that someone was being hunted by the police would be sure to open ears and loosen tongues. Now, you admit that you lied to the police. Also, you claim, and I believe you, that you don't normally lie. Is that right?"

"Yes, ma'am. I'm sorry."

"Well, now we come to the crux of the matter. Why did you lie? Were you trying to cover up criminal behavior, like Carly? Or, were you just playing some stupid game here at Elm Hill? If it's the first, you and Carly will be sleeping in the same cell tonight. If it's the second, we don't care about it, but you need to convince me that that's the case. Let's start by discussing your conversation with Amy Strong. Was there anything in it that made you lie?"

"There wasn't anything out of the ordinary in our first conversation that I just told you about. We had a long talk that evening, however. She gave me a lot of good and helpful information about what my duties would be and answered my questions about how to handle and care for the patients there. Then she told me that I needed to look out for Andy Russell because he was spying on the ward and trying to get Miss Rayburn in trouble. She said all the staff on the ward were scared that something bad would happen to them because they're loyal to Miss Rayburn. This scared me because I don't want to be involved in that kind of situation. I was afraid that people would be looking at me closely to see which side I'm on."

"Is this why you said earlier that you lied because you were scared?"

"Yes ma'am."

"So lots of people on the Violent Ward hate Andy and want to get him in trouble?"

"That's what Miss Strong said. I haven't talked to anyone else about him."

"Why are you so deferential to her? For example, you call her 'Miss Strong.' Isn't she just a nurses' aide?"

"She has a very strong personality. Clearly, she's the most important of the nursing students and aides. Most of the girls look up to her or are scared of her. I don't want to get involved in hospital politics. I feel good when I help my patients, but I'm don't like contentious situations."

"Well, I'm a little sensitive about talk about spying on the Violent Ward. Do you know Emma Hughes?"

"Yes, of course. We both live in Brackman. She's sweet and very good with her patients. We're friends."

"Emma is my friend, too, after we met on this investigation. So, I don't like people who give her trouble. Somebody complained to the police that she had tried to interfere with and spy on the Violent Ward regarding Carrie Adams.

"You see then why I'm skeptical about gossip about spying on the Violent Ward. Getting the police involved in hospital politics is disgusting, but I don't think you're involved."

"I agree with you ma'am that it's bad, but I don't know anything more about what's happening on the Violent Ward."

"Okay, I believe you. I've got one last topic for questioning. You were almost shocked yesterday when I asked you about your rubber apron. I need to figure out what its significance is. I see you're wearing yours now. Why? I thought you only wore it for dealing with messy patients."

"Yes, ma'am. That's right, but I was a little traumatized by getting a bedpan dumped over me yesterday. I guess I kept it on today to feel secure and didn't think to take it off when you called me up here."

"That makes sense. I can certainly sympathize with your being upset. I hate it when a prisoner vomits on me. Maybe I should get an apron to wear when I'm dealing with drunks. Still, that doesn't explain why you looked so scared. Are you going to tell me?"

"I thought you knew what he did to me."

"Andy did something to you? That's hard to believe, especially the way that you were handling him in that restraining belt."

"No, it wasn't Andy, of course. It was that awful creep, Dr. Carmichael. I was talking to one of his patients, Miss Delaware, in the day room yesterday morning, when he came up and asked if we could consult about her in private. Actually, I was flattered that a doctor would be interested in what I thought. He took me to her room for privacy and to show me something. When he closed and locked the door behind us, however, he leered at me and said that 'Your black rubber apron makes your titties irresistible.' Then he reached out and fondled me. This was the most humiliating thing that ever happened to me, except perhaps being handcuffed. I started to cry, and he let me out of the cell with a pat on my fanny. When you asked about the apron, I thought that someone had seen us through the observation window and was gossiping to the whole ward."

"That's awful. I'm so sorry for you. Are you going to complain?"

"I don't think so. Doctors are so powerful that he might be able to get me into trouble. Now, at least, I'll know not to let him close to me."

"I think that he's disgusting, but without other witnesses or physical signs of abuse, I don't think that I could arrest him. Now, I'm going to have a couple of people listen to this. I'm going to ask Andy to come watch you while you wait. You shouldn't be alone."

We heard the door to the conference room open, and Miss Mason whispered that I should go meet Laura. I wended my way through the corridors of the administrative suite and met her in front of Denise's office. The two secretaries looked up at us from their work but seemed afraid to ask us what was happening. Laura led me down the corridor to the conference room and stopped about halfway down its fifty-foot length.

"Hi, Andy. Do you have any questions?"

"No. Actually, I feel pretty sorry for the girl unless there's something I don't know."

"I would guess that she's just scared of Amy and didn't mean any harm. I'm off to play the recording for Miss Rayburn. It will be interesting to see how she responds. Helga is still cuffed to her chair so she shouldn't be any trouble. Try to keep her calm if you can. You shouldn't be threatening to her."

Helga looked up when I entered the conference room. She wasn't crying anymore but looked forlorn, like Carly had before her arrest. I walked over to her, patted her gently on the back, and sat down next to her on the side where her right hand was still handcuffed to her chair. Suddenly, a look of alarm crossed her face.

"Oh, Andy. You heard, didn't you? You know what I did."

"That's all right, Helga. Amy is really mean. She seems to hate Carly and me. You probably should be scared of her. There is one thing, I'm not spying on Miss Rayburn or trying to get anyone in trouble. I know so little about a psychiatric hospital and am so busy with my specific duties that there's not much I can say about the ward. I've seen that Miss Rayburn is a very good manager."

"Please don't hate me."

"I like you, Helga. Really, I'm sorry for you."

"If that's true, will you hold me for a minute? I'm so scared. I'm in such big trouble."

She managed to stand awkwardly in her handcuffs, and we hugged for several minutes. Then she sat down and smiled wanly at me.

"Thank you. I don't think that I can get much comfort from very many other people."

"Don't think like that, Helga. I know you feel so alone now, but I'm sure you have lots of friends. I was just talking to Mrs. Ward and she told me that the patients on Ward 2 love you. You've done so many good things. In terms of being in trouble, Officer Sanders didn't release you, but she didn't sound like she was going to arrest you, either."

"I don't think I'm worried about being arrested. There isn't anything beyond what I told her. It's my situation here that's ruined. Everyone knows that you're Miss Mason's protégé. Since I tried to spy on you, that means that I was spying on her. If she fires me, I don't know what I'll do. Even if I don't get fired without a reference, I'm sure that I'll be severely punished. I'll be lucky if I only get toilets for two weeks. I feel so alone and frightened."

"I've heard about doing toilets as punishment. What does it actually mean?"

"Instead of working your regular shift, you have to clean toilets and bathrooms on your hands and knees for a day or more. You have to wear attendants' coveralls, kneepads, rubber gloves, and an apron. You can't take them off until the shift is over, so everyone knows you're in disgrace. Miss Mason doesn't impose it to anywhere near the extent that Miss Lattimore did when she was the Director of Nursing, but I know that I've been bad."

I didn't know what to do, so I took her hand. We sat in silence for several minutes until the door opened and Laura came in with Miss Rayburn. She looked a little surprised, perhaps because we were holding hands. I got up and turned to leave, but Miss Rayburn cut me short.

"Don't go, Andy. I'm glad you're here. I want you to hear what I have to say to Helga.

"I've got several points to go over with you, Helga. First, you did something that is very, very bad for a nurse. You lied to someone in authority. You have to tell doctors and your nurse supervisors the exact truth. If you don't, your patients could be harmed. A policewoman shouldn't be any different. We've had some horrible things happen at Elm Hill in the last few weeks. Consequently, we need to give the police all our help to make sure that the criminals are caught and punished so that they can't threaten our good work.

"Second, Emma and Andy aren't doing bad things. I don't know how Amy got that into her head. She's very loyal to me and to the ward, which I appreciate. Still, I'm not worried about spying. Have you seen anything bad in your two days on the ward?"

"No, ma'am. All I see are people working hard to keep our patients cared for in very trying circumstances."

"Well, you know much more about nursing than Andy. How is he going to know even what to look for? Look at it another way. If you say that you want to prevent someone from spying on our ward, aren't you implying that there's something major going on? Do you understand what I'm saying, Helga."

"Yes, ma'am. I know that you're a very good Nurse Manager and very well respected. I guess that Amy just got me confused. I'm sorry."

"You have nothing to be sorry about. You were put in a position that you shouldn't have been in. My last point is that you have been an exceptional student nurse. You're talented and dedicated. You should be proud of what you've accomplished."

Miss Rayburn then walked over to Helga, lifted her from her chair, and hugged her. Without another word she turned and left the room. As the door was closing, Laura stepped over to Helga.

"Helga, from all I've learned, there's no reason to suspect you of any criminal act or to arrest you. I'm sorry that you had to be handcuffed, but your needless lie made you a suspect. Here, let me release you. Please wait. Miss Mason wants to talk to you."

Laura then walked over to the tape recorder at the end of the table, took out the tape, and put it into her purse. Helga sat down and took my hand again, looking very scared and clutching me tightly. The door opened and Miss Mason entered. She smiled at Laura who was heading for the door and came and sat at the conference table across from Helga, who was almost shivering.

"You're very frightened of me, Helga, aren't you? What do you think I'm going to do to you?"

"I know I was bad and have to be punished. I'm very sorry."

"I agree with Miss Rayburn that we can't tolerate lies. If I catch you in a lie like that again, I'll put you in the toilets for three weeks. Do you understand?"

"Yes, ma'am."

"Now, don't cry, girl. I'm not going to punish you for what you've done. I also agree with Miss Rayburn that you were put in an untenable position. Really, your lie wasn't that bad. You weren't covering up anything that was wrong. Miss Rayburn is probably talking to Amy already. If she asks you to do anything suspicious in the future, come to me immediately about it. Will you do that?"

"Yes, ma'am. Of course I will. Thank you. I thought you were going to destroy my life. My Mom and Dad would have been so ashamed of me."

"They should definitely be proud of you."

Chapter 21 ~ Financial Schemes

Miss Mason asked me to come back to her office. When we got there she asked Mrs. Holdstrom to get Mrs. Roberts and then bring a fresh pot of coffee. The two came back after about five minutes, bearing coffee and cookies.

"Welcome back, Melinda. I'm so sorry that you had to go through this horrible experience. Have you heard about that awful Dr. Matthews has been arrested? How are you and Billy? Gwen told me that you have something important to tell me, but let's hear about you first."

"Thank you so much for asking, ma'am. I appreciate how you stood up for me. Without your help, I'd still be in jail and Carl would have Billy all to himself. I also appreciate how kind the policewoman was to Billy. Instead of having him institutionalized, she took him to her sister. I was so ashamed to go back home, but it didn't turn out that badly. Three of the women he'd tried to seduce where watching and one of them snapped his picture when the policewoman led him out of the house in a strait jacket. I can't wait for the film to be developed. I hope that Billy and I will be fine. We're going into the program for abused wives and children that Dr. Harvey runs."

"I hope everything works out well for you. Many women in Dr. Harvey's program make good recoveries, but it can take a long time."

"Well, it's good you're done with police. Now, let's get to your other news. Did you find out something about our bookkeeping?"

"No, at least not directly, but I just learned something about First National that may be a little frightening. Billy and I were home last night. At about 7:30 there was a knock on the door. It was Joan McGuire, the girl who set up our account at First National. We got to be friends when I was working with her on the arrangements and have gone out to lunch together several times since then. I was surprised to see her but grateful that she evidently didn't think that I was an embezzler. I even cried a little just to see her."

"She gave me a hug and said she couldn't imagine how traumatic it must have been to be arrested. She knew that I must be innocent from working with me. She has a cousin who's a policeman, so she heard first that Carl had beaten Billy and me and had tried to blame me for his own crime. Then she found out that I had been released and wanted to come over and show her friendship. She had much more on her mind than a social visit, however. She had been a little troubled about something that happened at her bank. Consequently, when she found out about the fraudulent nature of our original account, she thought that Elm Hill needed to know that there might be something fishy going on at First National. One reason for her coming to visit was to ensure that nobody at First National would know that we were in touch.

"She had set up our account in December so that it would be ready to receive the funds from the state transfer at the beginning of January. It seemed routine, and she was glad that First National was finally getting some business from Elm Hill. In mid-February a woman came in with an authorization purportedly signed by Dr. Rydberg to transfer the funds to the Harrell Health Company. At the time she didn't think anything about it, but now she wonders, especially since she didn't know the woman and had never heard of Harrell Health.

"Then in March, Kenneth Ward, one of the Bank's managers, called her into his office. She hated him because he was mean to the staff and, in particular, liked to make the women employees feel uncomfortable. When she came to his office that day he leered at her and asked whether she thought that her sweater was too tight for business attire, which made her blush. Then he made her tell him all about the account that she had set up for Elm Hill. Finally, he told her that there would be a huge increase in the amount of funds going into the account in June and that she should set up a mechanism for the money to be directly transferred into the account of Reynolds Construction. She had thought that this was odd at the time, but once she learned that the account had already been used for criminal activities, she became frightened that she could be arrested for fraud.

"I told her that this was definitely scary. First, if we started having big diversions from the transfer payments that we get from the state, we won't be financially viable much longer. Second, Reynolds Construction hasn't had any projects for us for a long time. I checked with Dr. Rydberg this morning and there's nothing planned for the foreseeable future. We're not even contemplating anything that would involve them because they have a slightly unsavory reputation. If they're trying to get money from us, it's outright theft. There is some good news. We got our funds from the state yesterday, and all of them went into the hospital's normal account. Nobody can divert them unless Dr. Rydberg and I both authorize it, so the money seems safe. Finally, Dr. Rydberg closed our account with First National this morning, citing the Matthews scandal. That way, we're fully protected against anything that bank might try to do. Still, I'm scared that somebody tried to steal so much money from Elm Hill."

"Well, thanks so much for letting us know. The key questions are who's trying to steal from us and how in the world did they think they could get away with something so blatant."

Chapter 22 ~ A Graduation Surprise

I got the three o'clock bus from Osloville Thursday afternoon. Surprisingly, once the bus pulled out of the station, I didn't feel elation about my upcoming graduation, but rather a sense of relief that I was escaping the pressure cooker of the mysteries surrounding Elm Hill. Without realizing it, I must have gone from the excitement of being in the same ward with a notorious supposed murderess to the fear of possible threats from the murky murder conspiracy. I hadn't even had a chance to talk to Carrie since her aborted trip to the electro-shock suite. The only time that she was allowed out of her cell during our shift was when she was straitjacketed and escorted by Amy. I suddenly realized how brave and lonely she must be, which stiffened my resolve to help the Black Angels get to the bottom of the plots that were enveloping Elm Hill and keeping Carrie a prisoner.

I reached College City a few minutes after six. My family was waiting to pick me up. Mom and dad were proud of us and very pleased that both of us were graduating within two days of each other. We went to dinner at The Salzburg, a very good German restaurant on the other side of the city from the university. This was the first time that I'd eaten there, and I was quickly won over by the mouth-watering sauerbraten and the dessert pastries.

My family peppered me with questions about Elm Hill. Dad, of course, was interested in the medications that they used, but I couldn't satisfy his curiosity at all because only nurses were allowed to dispense them. Mom wanted to know what the patients were like and whether trying to care for them was dangerous. I told her that the senile dementia patients on Ward 2 were docile but that it was sad working with them because they had almost no hope of getting better. I didn't say how sprightly Mrs. Ward was because that would raise issues about unjustified committals that I didn't think my family was ready for. I then went on with some stories about the Violent Ward which included both some of the patients' less violent symptoms and an emphasis on how I had never felt threatened in my month of working there. Again, I thought that discretion was the better part of valor and didn't mention the special protective wear for dealing with messy patients.

My sister Jennifer, for her part, seemed fascinated by strait jackets and rampaging patients. She seemed disappointed when I told her that the popular image of howling straitjacketed patients was far overdrawn, even in our Violent Ward. However, she did perk up when I told her that I regularly put Jenny Sachs in a heavy restraining belt and escorted her for her exercise period and that I had once strapped Carrie Adams to a gurney and pushed her to an electro-shock session. I was slightly taken aback by my parents' evident satisfaction in the confinement and harsh treatment of poor Jenny, presumably because of their strong political support for her ex-husband.

Friday was very enjoyable. We slept late, and then I showed my family around campus. Although it was early June and sunny, the day wasn't hot and was nice for strolling. My dad got excited when we went through the Pharmacy School and both my parents were quite interested to tour the Department of Psychology's facilities in Washington Hall. I introduced them to Linda Harding, the head secretary, who regaled them with my academic accomplishments, confirmed my meeting with Dr. Calder at 3:00, and asked how I liked working in a psychiatric hospital. Jennifer bragged that I had prime responsibility for keeping the crazed former wife of Rodney Sachs restrained and controlled, which impressed Linda, made my mother wince, and brought me regret that I couldn't tell them about the more complex reality of Jenny's life.

I met with Dr. Calder in her office where we relaxed in comfortable chairs, sipped coffee, and nibbled small Swedish pastries. She started out by asking me to describe what I had been doing at Elm Hill and what I had learned from it. She looked slightly disappointed when I told them that the pressure of my daily duties of coping with the patients on the Violent Ward made it hard to comprehend what was happening in the broader institution. Then I moved on to what was happening at Elm Hill. This flabbergasted her. After just a quick synopsis of the Carrie Adams mystery, Dr. Calder rang Linda and said that our meeting was being extended and that she shouldn't be disturbed unless the President of the University wanted her. Then she turned to me.

"Andy, I can't believe it. Should I get you out of there? I certainly didn't mean for you to face personal danger. What does Miss Mason think is going on? Should I call her now?"

"Don't call her at Elm Hill. The hospital operators are notorious for eavesdropping and gossiping. Really, I want to stay. I was just thinking about poor Carrie on the bus ride over here, how terribly alone and frightened she must be. I want to be part of helping her."

"Thanks for the warning. I'll be circumspect, but I need to talk with her."

She then called Linda again and asked her to contact Miss Mason at the Elm Hill Psychiatric Hospital in Osloville.

"Hello. I'm so glad I could reach you, Carol. How are you? That's good. Next week after graduation, I'm starting a two-week vacation to Canada, so I'll be driving through Osloville. Is there any chance that I can meet you and, perhaps, tour Elm Hill. I'd love to hear any ideas that you might have for collaborating with the University."

Professor Calder listened for a minute or two and then responded. "That's fantastic. I'll have my secretary make the hotel reservations for Wednesday and Thursday nights. We can meet for breakfast on Thursday morning at nine. It will be great to see you."

The phone rang again almost as soon as Dr. Calder put it down. "My goodness, does the President want me?" When she picked it up, she looked even more surprised and motioned for me to take it. "Linda says the police are trying to find you."

I took the phone with a little puzzlement and trepidation, but was quickly rewarded with Laura's voice that was almost bubbling. "Hi, Andy. I guess I'm a good detective. I got your parents' motel from Gwen. Luckily they were there taking a nap and told me about your appointment at the Psychology Department. We thought that we might be transporting Missy the Mistress back tomorrow, but she's been treated so badly here that she wants to leave right away. So, the matron's getting her chained up right now. Why I'm calling you is that it isn't that much longer to follow the U.S. highway up through College City than to go on State Route 3, which is slower and more dangerous driving. We should get to College City about 5:30. We'll stop there for supper at Ryan's Diner, which the hotel recommended. We'd love for you to join us. Incidentally, your sister will be there. She answered the phone when I called the hotel and got all excited when I said that I was a policewoman."

"That's great news, Laura. I'll be very happy to meet you. By the way, my advisor is more than a little worried about all the criminal activity surrounding Elm Hill."

"I'll see you at the restaurant. Let me talk to her for a minute."

I handed the phone back to Dr. Calder who listened without comment, then said goodbye with a smile.

I went back to the hotel at five and Jennifer was waiting for me with more anticipation than I could ever remember. Since she was dressed so nicely, I put on a sport coat and a tie. We got to the restaurant a few minutes before 5:30 and waited outside for about five minutes until an Osloville police car pulled up. Laura got out and the matron in her mid-forties emerged from the passenger's side. Laura stepped forward and, much to my surprise, gave me a light hug, while the matron removed her shackled prisoner from the car. I had expected Missy to be young. Instead she was about thirty. A newspaper I had read at the library after lunch had described her as a "blonde bombshell," but her unkempt hair, lack of make-up, and black-and-white striped detention dress had definitely cut into her attractiveness. The matron took her to the restroom while the rest of us were seated and ordered cheeseburgers and sodas.

As the waitress left, Laura patted Jennifer on the arm. "I'm so glad to meet you. I like your brother. Would you like to be a policewoman? This is the most satisfying part of the job, escorting a criminal to jail. This girl is almost as bad as the doctor, but I think she's given up now. She smashed an officer with a heavy briefcase when she was arrested, but now she's totally docile."

"I'm not sure I could be like you, but it does sound exciting. Do you arrest a lot of people? Do they resist and attack you often?"

Laura laughed. "Women are almost always cooperative and do what they're told. Men differ a lot. Some of them are more docile for a woman than a man, but many can't stand being in a woman's custody. I don't deal with male prisoners very often. When I do, I'm very strict until I know that they've become submissive."

Jennifer looked quite impressed, especially when Laura let her finger one of the pairs of handcuffs on her belt, leading me to wonder what her aspirations might be. The matron then brought Missy to the table, drawing marked glances from most of the other patrons and the two waitresses. Missy was seated next to me because, Laura said, she had a message for Miss Mason.

"The officers told me that you're very close to the Director of Nursing at the psychiatric hospital. After hearing about Max's other girls, I know I've been a fool. I may even have one of his hussies for a cellmate in Osloville. I hate Max. There's something your director should know. Max hated that head nurse and said that she was more stuck up than his wife, so I guess that I'd like to give her any help that I can. Max stole $50,000 in January and was planning to steal another $50,000 in June if nobody caught on. In late April, however, a man with a gun accosted him in a parking lot. He was muscular and had an evil-looking scar on this face. He told Max that he knew all about his scheme and that Max had better forget that it had ever happened because the *big boys* were taking it over. He then threatened to come back and strangle Max with one of 'his cute little nursies' stockings' if he ever squealed or tried to use that account again. Max was quite scared, so that was the end of our scheme."

When a waitress brought our drinks, Laura explained that they were transporting their prisoner from State Capital to Osloville. The cheeseburgers came right after that and we finished quickly, clearly to the relief of the waitresses. On our way out, Laura told me that Jennifer was coming to visit her for a week later in the summer and whispered that she had leant one of her pairs of handcuffs to Jennifer to practice with over the weekend and that I should bring them back with me on Tuesday.

My graduation late Saturday morning was solemn but so large that it was hard to get emotional about it. A girl next to me said that it was more for the parents than the graduates. Mom and Dad certainly seemed thrilled and even Jennifer was very happy for me and gave me a big hug. Her graduation Monday evening was a much smaller affair with just forty-three seniors flipping their tassels. I finally met her boyfriend Henry Jackson. He was a nice enough guy, handsome, and physically imposing. Still, I didn't envy him given Jennifer's weekend exposure to sorority rushes and policewomen.

Chapter 23 ~ Black Angel Business

The bus route back to Osloville was circuitous and involved two changes of buses. Although I left at 9:30, I didn't get back until a little after two. It had started to drizzle about halfway through the trip and by the time I reached Osloville it was raining quite hard. As I stepped off from the bus I heard my name called out from inside the station and looked up to see Mr. Jones waiting for me. Once I got inside the station, he pointed toward a bench where he had dropped my raingear. We shook hands and exchanged several jokes. He appeared to be in a jovial mood.

"Congratulations to the college graduate. How much longer before I have to start calling you doctor?"

"Thanks. My professor says that it should take four or five years to complete my PhD, but even then the psychiatrists wouldn't consider me a 'real' doctor. So, you, Ella, and my friends here can keep calling me Andy until the cows come home."

This made him chuckle. He said, "It's appropriate that you have to get into your rubber wardrobe this afternoon since there are several things for you to do as a Black Angel. The big thing is that we're having dinner at the Holdstroms' this evening to discuss what's going on at Elm Hill. Detective Perkins told Miss Mason that he has some things to discuss. Before that, you've got a chore. Could you give Mrs. Ward a visit and ask her a question for us?

"Ella is friends with Marcella Riker, who was the housekeeper for the Wards and stayed on after the Boltons bought the house. When the house was being sold, Marcella saw several boxes of papers being taken out of Mr. Ward's study. The butler and a mover who were carrying the boxes went out the backdoor but didn't drop the boxes in the garbage bin. Instead, they went out the back gate into the alley. They didn't drive away and they came back about fifteen minutes later. Marcella didn't think much about it at the time, but when Ella started telling her about the shenanigans that nasty Kenneth had got up to, she wondered if this might be important. Anyway, if you can see Mrs. Ward before we go to the Holdstroms', there's a small chance that you could find out something helpful."

Mrs. Ward wasn't expecting me and was overjoyed at the surprise. She congratulated me, reminisced about how she and Robert had enjoyed their college graduations so long ago, and then shared her good news that her new optometrist had given her a prescription for glasses that he was sure would allow her to read books with regular print. "Oh, Andy. I'm so happy."

Finally, I broached the subject of the documents in her husband's study. "I hadn't thought of this before, but it was a little strange. Robert never brought his work home. He had books in his study that he liked to read, but they were novels. He was also addicted to crossword puzzles and usually did a couple every evening that we stayed in. Then, a month or two before his death, he had a large filing cabinet moved into his office. I didn't pay much attention to what he was doing, but once when I went in to see him, he was working with bank documents instead of doing his crosswords. What caught my attention was that several of the documents were labeled First National, not Osloville, Bank. At the time, I thought he might be helping Kenny. Now, I wonder.

"I think I can help you with the mystery of where the documents might have been carted off to. Our property ran all the way back from the alley to the crest of the ridge, although that part was pretty much a tangle of trees and underbrush. Somewhere in there was a shed that we used to store equipment. After the war we expanded our garage and moved the stuff there, and the path to the shed was overgrown in a year. Mr. Redmond, our butler, knew about it and could have thought that taking something there at the last moment was better than just throwing it away. I doubt that Kenny or Meredith knew anything about the bank documents. If you can get permission to look, I might be even more helpful. When I came here, I brought my keys which the hospital is holding for me. Whatever Kenny says about my being gaga, I still remember which key fits which lock in my beautiful old home."

It was still raining when Mrs. Holdstrom picked me up at 5:30. She told us that we would have the house to ourselves. Her husband was having a business dinner downtown while the two children were across town dining with their aunt and uncle. Their housekeeper had been given the evening off after baking several large pans of lasagna for us.

By the time that we got there, everyone else had arrived. As we milled around in the entryway, I moved next to Laura and gave her the handcuffs and keys that I had brought back from Jennifer. She smiled and whispered so nobody else could hear, "Thanks, Andy. I think your sister is an aspiring policewoman. Did she practice on you?"

That made me blush. "Yes, she did it with my hands first in front of me and then behind me. She got pretty good by Tuesday morning in keeping me effectively restrained without hurting me. I hope you don't entice her away from college." This made her giggle.

We feasted on lasagna and ice tea and chatted without mentioning the case. When we were finished, we moved to the library where coffee and several large plates of pastries had been set out.

Detective Perkins smiled and said, "Let me start with our new prisoners. We thought we might have trouble with Dr. Matthews and his State Capital nurse, but thankfully we were wrong. After Mistress Missy sliced open a patrolman's face with their briefcase, they got a little, or more than a little, rough treatment. You should have seen the two matrons who brought Missy into the interview with us. They were as big and muscular as that attendant in the Violent Ward and, unlike her, looked mean and quite happy to use their muscles. Missy seemed so grateful that Laura and Emily didn't start slapping her around that she became totally cooperative. She agreed to confess and incriminate Matthews as long as we wouldn't make her go back to the State Capital jail. The jail captain was just as glad to get rid of her and provided the paperwork we needed far faster than I've ever seen a police bureaucrat work. Also, thanks for passing on what Joan McGuire of First National told Melinda about a woman getting the money from Elm Hill's account. We put Missy, Carly, Wendy Carter, and two policewomen into a line-up for Miss McGuire, and she identified Missy with no hesitation.

"Matt and I didn't get any trouble from Dr. Matthews when we hauled him back on Saturday, but we didn't get any cooperation or confession, either. He knows he's going away, and he's not going to do anything to help us. I don't think that he knows anything about the

Adams murder or other plots concerning Elm Hill. If he did, he should have squealed to save his own skin on the embezzlement. Of course, there's always the chance that he might be involved in something so bad that he can't admit to it. Still, I think that all he was after was money and sexy nurses. Since his wife controls the money, he may be sitting in jail before his trial, too. I expect that he's going to get a pretty high bail because of all the publicity.

"In addition, Missy's comment about Matthews being scared off by a big scar-faced thug made me thing of Lars Grogan, an enforcer for the Griggs gang. He wouldn't tell us anything. Still, an underworld connection to Elm Hill is a little scary."

Miss Mason agreed. "Well, Richard, that's in line with the growing unease at Elm Hill. Dr. Rydberg is growing suspicious that there's more going on than just the usual minor intrigues. Andy, did Mrs. Ward tell you anything of interest?"

I quickly summarized Ella's story and what Mrs. Ward said about her husband bringing banking papers that could involve First National home shortly before his death and about the possibility that they could have been stashed in a forgotten shed just before the Boltons moved in. This got Detective Perkins' interest, but he wasn't sure what he could do.

"It might be valuable if we could find out whether the papers are there and what they might contain, but I don't see how we can do it. No judge would grant a search warrant for River Ridge on the flimsy evidence that we have."

Miss Mason sounded positively chipper. "Don't be so pessimistic, Richard. The Boltons have no connection with the case and no reason to be interested in any old papers of the Wards. Dr. Rydberg, as Hospital Director, can be considered Mrs. Ward's guardian. With any luck he might be able to arrange something without anybody paying any attention to some old moldy boxes of paper. If we find something, do you want it?"

"Let us look at it, but keep it safe. Actually, come to think of it, Melinda and, if Peter's willing, the Osloville Bank accountants should be far more competent in going through financial records than anyone we've got."

Chapter 24 ~ The Secret Shed

My first day back on the Violent Ward was uneventful. When I finished my nurse's notes I headed up to Ward 2 where Mrs. Ward was still at lunch. Mrs. Maxwell and another nurse I knew only as Shirley invited me into the lunchroom for cake and coffee to celebrate my graduation. Mrs. Ward greeted me with an excited expression, but waited until we found a quiet corner to elaborate.

"Well, Andy. You certainly know how to get the ball rolling. I can't believe it. This morning Mrs. Lawrence took me to my room after breakfast so we could have a private conversation. She had me sign a paper requesting Dr. Rydberg to obtain those papers for me and asked me who our butler had been. Then, an hour before lunch, she came in the day room and said that everything's been arranged. You're to go down to Mrs. Holdstrom's office now to help out." I got a kiss on the check. "If something evil's being done, I'd feel really good if I can help stop it."

When I got to Mrs. Holdstrom's office she had gone to the cafeteria for lunch, but Clem and Melinda were waiting for me. They were obviously anticipating a tramp through the woods since they were wearing rubber boots and Clem had actually brought my boots from my room. He was in a jovial mood.

"Well, it looks like we're ready. Luckily, the old butler, Joseph Redmond, was easy to find. He was glad to see me. He thought that the files that Mr. Ward had brought home might be very important and didn't want them tossed out or sent to that nasty Mr. Kenneth. So, at the last moment, he got the idea to put them in the old shed. His big problem was that after Mrs. Ward was removed so suddenly, he didn't have anyone to tell where they were. He's excited that something might finally be done. I hope that we're not disappointed in what we find."

The drive to River Ridge was uneventful. For most of the twenty minutes in the car, Clem and I quizzed Melinda about the dangers to Elm Hill's finances. On this question at least, she could be reassuring. That morning, Dr. Rydberg had issued a directive that any financial transaction over $200 had to be signed by both himself and Melinda. He also had set up a meeting with Peter Holdstrom to work out an agreement that would make Osloville Bank our sole financial agent and give them increased auditing powers to make sure that hospital funds were not mismanaged. In fact, Mr. Holdstrom had agreed to let Melinda work with one of his top accountants that afternoon if we found anything suspicious in the Boltons' shed.

We went up the back way to River Ridge and parked behind the Boltons' mansion. When we got out of the car, Clem opened the trunk and, evidently expecting a messy walk through the woods, passed out raincoats and rubber helmets even though the day was sunny. He then asked me to go to the back door of the house and get the maid who was supposed to accompany us. My knock was quickly answered by a woman in a blue uniform and green rubber gloves. She seemed to be in her 50s and looked pretty spry. She smiled and said, "Hi. I'm Marcella Riker. Seeing the way you're dressed, I guess I should get something to keep my uniform and shoes from being messed up. Even so, this should be a welcome change from polishing the silver. Both Mrs. Bolton and I think it's pretty exciting to discover a secret shed on the property."

After I introduced myself, she went back into the house and quickly returned wearing a rain bonnet and a well-worn tan cloth raincoat. She was delighted to meet Clem because she and Ella were good friends. Apparently, they especially liked to share gossip. We found the beginning of an old path on the far side of the alley, and Clem cleared it a little for us with a small scythe. After getting off the path a couple of times and probably covering fifty yards, we reached a decrepit shed that was half covered in vines. Clem approached the door, pulled an oil can from his raincoat pocket, and squirted it on the key. It took several applications of oil and some straining on his part, but he got the door open and handed the key to Marcella, who seemed delighted.

"Oh, thank you, Clem. Both Mrs. Bolton and I were entranced when we read *The Secret Garden* as teenagers. A secret shed doesn't sound so romantic, but maybe we can find some secrets here."

The shed was about twelve feet wide and a little deeper. It had windows on each side that by some miracle hadn't been broken, but even on a sunny day the surrounding woods didn't let in much light. Clem needed to use a powerful flashlight in order to see what the interior held. Two sturdy wooden boxes had been stacked near the door. There were a rusty lawnmower and bicycle at the rear, along with some gardening implements hanging on the wall. In addition, a six-foot long bench had been built along the left side. Clem grabbed the top box and carted it to the bench, and I followed with the second. The tops had been nailed down, but Clem, who had seemingly thought of everything, produced a short pry bar and opened them with no trouble. Both were about half filled with papers that appeared to have survived their storage. He started to turn away, but then stopped, pulled at the bench, and looked at the flooring under it.

"Here, Melinda. Why don't you see if there's anything of interest in the boxes. Then we'll try to find a secret for Marcella and Mrs. Bolton."

We waited for about fifteen minutes while Melinda shuffled through the papers in first one box and then the other. When she was finished, she turned toward us with a slight smile.

"I can't be certain, but I think that what's here is consistent with the supposition that Mr. Ward was going over records that might indicate some financial problems. The first box has materials on the personal accounts of Kenneth Ward and Gene Simmons for 1951 and the first half of 1952. There are some records from Osloville Bank, especially concerning the Trust Fund that Mr. Ward set up for his children, but most of them are from First National. To me, this suggests that someone there must have supplied the records without going through proper channels, which was probably illegal. There are some large amounts going into and out of their accounts, but then they're fairly rich bankers. The other box has papers about the accounts that Reynolds Construction, Maverick Motors, and Ernst Real Estate had with First National from January through March 1952. I don't know enough about their businesses to know whether or not there's anything suspicious, but in both boxes there are some transactions underlined in red."

"Congratulations, Melinda. There's nothing definite, but I think that you should make an appointment with the accountant at Osloville Bank for later this afternoon.

"Now, Marcella, let's see if we can find a secret for you. The bench felt like it can be swung away from the wall, and there's a dirty drop cloth under it that could hide something. Here, Andy. Let's move the boxes out of the way."

Once we'd moved them, Clem pulled at one end of the bench, swung it away from the wall, and then kicked away the extremely dirty drop cloth, revealing a trap door in the wooden flooring. He pulled it up and shone his flashlight into the space below.

"There's a small room down here with some boxes and piles of stuff. Given the amount of grime on it, it looks like it's been there a lot longer than two years. Well, Marcella. Here's a mystery for the Boltons. If they want the police to look at it, have them call Detective Richard Perkins since he's investigating something that may be related to that stash."

"Oh, Clem. How thrilling. I'll get Mrs. Bolton to send me on an errand to the Rowe house where Ella's working, if you don't mind me telling her before you do."

"Go ahead, Marcella. You deserve the pleasure. Ella and I can enjoy talking about our kids tonight."

While Clem and I put the boxes in the trunk of our car, Melinda went into the house with Marcella to call Osloville Bank. She came back about five minutes later, looking very happy. She had talked with Jim McDermott, the bank's Chief Accountant, who had told her to bring the boxes to the bank so they could go over them together. Mrs. Bolton got excited about her "secret shed" and, after checking with her husband, had called Detective Perkins who would be coming over later in the afternoon.

We dropped Melinda and the boxes at Osloville Bank and returned to Elm Hill. Mrs. Holdstrom told us that Miss Mason wanted to see us at 4:00. I went up to Ward 2 to read to Mrs. Ward for what we hoped would be the last time since her new glasses were supposed to be ready the next Monday. Instead of reading, however, we talked in low voices about our trip to her old home. She was pleased and excited that she might have helped us find something useful and asked if I could get a copy of *The Secret Garden* for her to read the next week since she had loved it when it was first published.

When I got to Mrs. Holdstrom's office, Clem was there alone. Within a couple of minutes Mrs. Holdstrom returned and asked us to go to Miss Mason's office where we found a carafe of coffee and a large plate of fresh strudel on the conference table. Miss Mason seemed in a very good mood.

"Thank you, Gwen for bringing the refreshments and taking the message from Melinda. Why don't you be the bearer of good tidings to Clem and Andy?"

"Certainly, Melinda called about three. The Osloville Bank's Chief Accountant had gone through the documents that you had brought in and found some very suspicious activities. Since the Trust Fund for the Ward children was set up in his bank, he had complete information about it. It's clear that, unless someone forged his name, Kenneth Ward took $15,000 from the Trust Fund to which he wasn't entitled. Whether that's criminal or not might be in a gray area, but he certainly doesn't look good. The First National accounts show that Ward and his brother-in-law Gene Simmons were playing with a lot more money than they should have had access to. In particular, each received payments of over $10,000 from Reynolds Construction and then seemingly used it to purchase stock. Furthermore, Reynolds, Ernst Realty, and Maverick Motors were moving far more money around among themselves than would appear normal.

"They didn't know what to do with the First National materials, however. Since they have no business having them, Mr. McDermott didn't think that it was a good idea to approach the other bank to get help in figuring out what was going on in those accounts. Luckily when Melinda called to give me the news about what they'd found, I got inspired. I was able to reach Detective Perkins at the police station. He and Detective Kempton had just returned from the Bolton house where they found liquor and guns under the old shed. They're pretty sure it's from Prohibition, so they're not very confident that they can do much with the evidence.

"Detective Perkins got excited when I told him about what Melinda and Mr. McDermott had found. He said that if the police took custody of the papers, they could go to First National and demand an explanation for the suspicious transactions. While the bank might complain a little, he thought that its upper management would probably be pleased to have a couple of crooks exposed as long as they didn't find out that their major rival had had access to records that reflected badly on them. Right now, Detective Perkins and a police accountant are working with Mr. McDermott to establish what's in those files. Peter, by the way, is almost ecstatic that he's being able to help the Wards. He really liked Robert and Betty and is horrified by the idea of bank fraud anywhere."

After we heard Mrs. Holdstrom's cheery recitation, the strudel tasted even better than usual.

Chapter 25 ~ A Wild Arrest

Laura came to Elm Hill the next evening to go over the personnel records of people who worked in the Violent Ward to see if she could find any links to the Griggs gang or the suspect businesses. About nine o'clock Miss Mason treated us both to donuts in the cafeteria, and Laura confessed that her search had proven fruitless. She had not found anyone who had held suspicious jobs before coming to Elm Hill or who seemed to be married or related to known gangsters or people with shady reputations. In contrast, Miss Mason appeared to be quite pleased with Dr. Calder's visit to Elm Hill.

"We had a wonderful visit, Andy. We caught up with each other this morning during the longest breakfast that I've ever had. I'm so happy and proud that someone like her has a good opinion of me. Then we spent three hours touring Elm Hill. She seemed impressed that our smaller size, larger staff, and specialization in patients allow us to provide much better treatment for the mentally ill than the state hospitals. She suggested that the hospital work with a couple of foundations to examine and develop better treatment regimens and that the two of us go to Chicago later this summer for some meetings with potential donors. Dr. Rydberg invited us to his house for mid-afternoon coffee. She's already agreed to incorporate us into her funded project for next year. That way, you can come back and do research here next summer if you want. Finally, she's more than a little worried about you, but she laughed about Laura. Evidently, she asked Laura during a telephone conversation whether you were in danger and Laura retorted that anyone who threatened you would get her weapon in their face. You seem to have a guardian angel." This made Laura blush, but she looked quite happy.

When we had finished with our snack, I walked Laura to her patrol car and then started back toward Brackman. I had hardly got out of the parking lot when she pulled up beside me. I opened the front passenger door and looked in inquiringly.

"Jump in. Oh, Andy. It's so exciting. When Richard and Matt went to arrest Ward this evening, they caught Kenny boy in bed with two women, his housekeeper and a bank teller. The slut of a housekeeper smacked Matt's face. I'm going to love throwing her in my cage. The bank teller had some incriminating documents with her, so she's going to jail, too."

It was less than a ten-minute drive to Ward's house in a prosperous community a little south and east of Elm Hill. When we got there, a patrol car and Detective Perkins' sedan were parked in the driveway. When we got out, Laura told me to wait by her car and open the door to the cage in the back when she brought "the tart" out. A young policeman was leaning on his patrol car and stifled a laugh as Laura strode purposefully past him.

"Too bad you missed the show. We got to see all of them in their garter belts. He had both the chicks in bed at the same time. Nobody answered the doorbell, but since the detectives had an arrest warrant, we pried open the back door and followed the giggles to the master bedroom on the second floor. That maid is really feisty. She slapped poor Matt Kempton and got handcuffed to a bedpost. Then she tried to kick me, so I cuffed her ankles together. I think that she's high on something besides alcohol. Laura may have her hands full getting her to headquarters."

That prophecy turned out to be a false one. When Laura emerged, she had full control over a lithesome teenage blonde in a black maid's uniform that seemed to have been designed for bedroom frolics rather than the duties of dusting. Her hands were cuffed behind her, and someone had replaced the handcuffs on her ankles with regular leg chains. Laura forced her forward while the maid swore at her somewhat incoherently. Detectives Perkins and Kempton and the other patrolman followed, savoring the spectacle. I got the door open and Laura pushed her in so hard that she hit the mesh screen in the middle of the back seat.

"Thanks, Andy. That crazy bitch bit me. I'll need a tetanus shot. I wish I were like Miss Mason and had a gag for out-of-control prisoners."

Detective Kempton came up, kissed her on the back of the neck, and then kissed her bitten wrist. They went back to the house, and Laura returned with her second prisoner a couple of minutes later. This woman was in her late twenties with light permed hair and a pretty face. She was wearing what would have been a nice suit except that the jacket, blouse and skirt were all wrinkled, her make-up was smeared, and one of her stockings was slipping down her leg. Unlike the maid, she seemed to be totally cooperative. She and Laura were cuffed wrist to wrist, and she followed her guard submissively. Laura had me open the front passenger door, seated her prisoner gently on the seat, and re-cuffed her hands through the inside door handle.

"Thanks, Andy. Here's a little tape recorder, please turn it on if I can get her talking. Richard thinks that she may be ready to confide in a woman. Sit behind me in the back. I'm pretty sure that our whacko maid won't be able to bite you through the thick mesh."

In point of fact, the wild prisoner was now half passed out, so I could turn my full attention to what was happening in the front seat. The woman was crying, and Laura patted her on the shoulder.

"I know this is terrible for you. What's your name?"

"Janie Wright. I'm so ashamed. I'm so ashamed."

"Are you married? I don't see a wedding ring. If you're not married, it might not be so bad."

"My jerk of a husband left me two years ago. I have a five year-old daughter who's staying with my mom and dad tonight. I told them I was having a late business meeting. Now I'm ruined."

"How did you ever get tangled up with Kenneth Ward?"

"He started paying attention to me about a year ago. I was flattered. A lot of the girls are frightened of him, but I don't mind letting him play with me. I hate to admit it, but I enjoy the sex. I don't even mind going to bed with him and Hilary together, which they obviously love."

"Are you embezzling money from the bank with him? The detectives say that they found incriminating documents in your briefcase."

"Oh, no, ma'am ... no. I've never stolen anything. Please believe me. What I've done is handle some big checks that come in for Mr. Ward and Mr. Simmons. They told me it wasn't illegal."

"Well, Janey, don't tell the detectives that I told you, but I definitely think you need to get a lawyer before you talk to them. Can your parents get you a lawyer? Make sure it's someone who can protect you from Ward and Simmons. I think that the detectives and the State's Attorney will be very lenient with you if you help them put those two crooks away."

We reached the police station without any other conversation of note. Janey had stopped crying, and Hilary had started snoring. Laura went around to the back, removed Hilary, and half dragged her now unresisting form into the jail entrance. A couple of minutes later a matron came out to escort Janey. About ten minutes later, Laura came out and opened my door.

"Hi, Andy. Isn't this exciting? Can I have the tape recorder? I need to leave it for Richard and Matt when they finally get the *bad boy banker* down here. The jerk demanded to see his lawyer before leaving his house. He's such a big shot that they figured that they should accommodate him, but the lawyer won't save him from the cells and a strip search. In fact, Richard is going to try to get the State Attorney's office to make sure he stays in jail an extra day or two."

"Here's the tape. Are they going to interrogate her now?"

"No, I'm sure they'll wait until morning. What they're excited about is that they now have documents directly from First National that will justify an investigation of their accounts. I don't think that the bank will try to protect corrupt employees. They're pretty sure that Ward, like Hilary, will test positive for drugs. That alone should be enough for a year or two in the state pen.

"Now, I'll give you a ride back to Elm Hill. I called Emma and she said that she could give me a tetanus shot since they have some vaccine on hand for patients and staff who cut themselves. I've agreed to give Matron Rawlings a ride home when their shift ends in a couple of minutes since her car's in the shop."

She then walked off toward the front of police headquarters, presumably to go to the detectives' office. A few minutes later, a woman in her late thirties came over to our car, got into the passenger seat, and turned back toward me.

"Hello, I'm Matron Rawlings. You must be Andy Russell. Laura tells that you're working at Elm Hill as Miss Mason's assistant. Do you like Osloville?"

"Yes, ma'am, but I've been too busy at the hospital to get to know the area. It's the first time that I've been up north."

At this point, Laura returned and started the car. The tenor of the conversation changed immediately, as the two women became excited and giggly.

"Laura, you said you had a very entertaining story for us."

"Oh, Marian. You wouldn't believe it. When I got there, they had all three of them handcuffed to different bedposts. That nasty maid was as you see her, except without any panties. The bank girl was wearing a black bra, garter belt and stockings. The real surprise was Ward who was in a woman's garter belt and nylons, too. What a sight. Maybe, they'll put him in with the women."

Matron Rawlings laughed. "Well, maybe that's the next extension of our duties. My news for you, Laura, is that the damn maid woke up when I was getting her chained and started kicking up another ruckus. I left her for Dora the Bully and her nightstick. Maybe that will knock some sense into her."

Chapter 26 ~ A Fright on the Night Shift

This week marked the end of a Monday-Friday cycle in our shift. For the next two weeks we were scheduled to be on duty Wednesday through Sunday. Instead of having a long break, however, I had been substituted for a male attendant on the night shift for Saturday and Sunday to make up for two of the three days I had missed during my long graduation weekend. When I went on duty Saturday night, therefore, I was hoping that the nighttime duties wouldn't be too arduous. Since all the patients were in their rooms, Molly Wells, the charge nurse for this shift, took us into the dining area for a leisurely snack of coffee and cream donuts over which she assigned our duties. In addition to me, the two female attendants were Sheila Mills, a Negro in her sixties and who was a close friend of Clem's, and April Gibbs, a pretty but sour-faced girl in her early twenties. I quickly got the impression that she was one of the new attendants whose attitude did not live up to Clem's standards. The three of us were supposed to mop the floors and public spaces and scrub the bathrooms later in the night. Before that, April was assigned to check the inventory in the two storerooms, while Sheila and I were supposed to check all the patient rooms, which was basically to make sure that there were no commotions going on in any of their darkened interiors.

I went out to the locker room in the entry hall to get my rubber work gloves and started checking the empty cells near the main entrance at the beginning of my round. As I glanced through the observation window for the second room to the left, I got a shock. The light was on. I pushed the door open rapidly and caught a nurse trying to push something under the mattress of the bed. She gave a little shriek as the door opened and turned to face me with an expression of fear. It was Rachel Weiss, the charge nurse from the previous shift. Something about her made me take command of the situation, as I would with a sneaky patient.

"What do you have? Show it to me. Now," I shouted.

She started to cry but reached back down, clumsily retrieved a magazine from under the mattress of the bed, and held it out toward me. It clearly was pornography with a picture of two muscular men wearing nothing but G-strings on the cover.

"What have you done? Down on the bed on your stomach. Put your hands and your feet by the restraints." I quickly locked first her right and then her left wrist to the bed and, more leisurely, secured her ankles.

"Why did you do it, Rachel? Are you trying to destroy Miss Mason?"

"I'm so sorry. I'm so ashamed." She turned her head away from me and started to cry again.

"I can't believe it. I thought you were nice. You're worse than Carly. I'm going to call Miss Mason."

Rachel kept her face turned away. I went back to the nurse's station where there was a telephone. Luckily, Mrs. Wells had gone into the administrative suite to do paperwork. I could call without trying to make up an acceptable explanation.

"Hello, Betty. Could you please connect me to Miss Mason's room? Hello, Miss Mason. I'm sorry to disturb you, but I just found something strange in Room 23. Are you interested?"

"I can be there in ten minutes. I'm sure that you wouldn't have called unless you thought it was important that I see it immediately."

I went back to the cell. Rachel still lay with her face to the wall but had stopped crying.

"Rachel, Miss Mason will be here in about ten minutes."

"Please, Andy. I know you must despise me, but could you do me a favor. I know I have to stay like this. I need a diaper. Please don't make me humiliate myself. You can do it without unlocking my wrist restraints."

"Sure, Rachel. I know how to diaper a patient. Certainly, I'll do it if you think you need it."

Actually, her diapering helped pass the time. I had just finished when Miss Mason entered and addressed her in a business-like tone.

"Well, Rachel. You're in trouble, aren't you? Where are your nurse's notes? I need to see what else you've been up to."

"Today's and yesterday's are in the cabinet behind the nurses' station. Miss Rayburn won't collect them until she comes on duty on

Monday. The key is the small bronze one on my keychain. Why do you need to see them? I'm not a bad nurse."

"Hush, Rachel. I need to know more about you before I can decide what to do with you. You understand that, don't you?"

"Yes ma'am."

Miss Mason left and then returned with a file that was thicker than I would have expected. Obviously, Miss Weiss was quite conscientious about her notes. Miss Mason read for perhaps ten minutes, flipping from one page to another in the file. Finally, she seemed satisfied.

"Rachel, I can see some major differences between what you do. How can you explain your notes on Carrie Adams in Room 13? I find them totally unsatisfactory."

The girl turned toward Miss Mason and started to cry again. "Oh, please, ma'am. I'm not a bad nurse. Please look at my notes for my other patients. I try to be conscientious. I really do. It's doctor's orders for Carrie Adams. Dr. Carson ordered me not to have contact with her. It's not my fault. Please, ask him."

"Well, if the charge nurse can't treat her, who can? Are you saying that Miss Rayburn personally handles her all the time during your shift? Don't be ridiculous. She's not even there after five. It clearly doesn't happen on the morning shift."

"No, ma'am. Please believe me. It's an attendant, Shannon Krebs, who takes care of her. I don't know why. She gives her notes directly to Miss Rayburn. Please, ask anyone on our shift. They'll tell you."

I saw Miss Mason's face change from grim to smiling at this response. "Well, Rachel. I actually believe you. You're too smart to tell a lie that could be easily disproved. However, we still have your pornography. Why did you bring it in here and hide it? Isn't that something some of the girls tape to the back of toilets in Brackman?"

"Please, ma'am. I didn't bring it here. I haven't used pornography before. I'm a shy girl, but I haven't done it. I inspected all the rooms today, even the vacant ones. I know that this one hasn't been used for at least six months. I found this under the mattress. I put it back and came in here at the end of my shift. I'm lonely. Andy caught me just as I was finishing. I didn't bring it here, though. I wouldn't even know where I could buy a magazine like that."

"Do you have any idea how long this filth has been here, Rachel? Please tell the exact truth. This is very important."

"I inspect the rooms about once a week. I'm almost certain that it wasn't here last Wednesday."

Miss Mason's visage had now turned kindly. She walked over to Rachel and stroked her hair gently.

"Rachel, Rachel. Why are you in restraints?"

"Because you're taking me into custody for masturbation?"

"That's not illegal. We've learned that some very bad people are trying to get the hospital in trouble. Andy, I presume, thought that you were smuggling contraband into the hospital to make it look like we're criminals. That's why he got mad at you.

"Andy, please unlock her restraints."

Once her wrists and ankles were free, Rachel sat up. She had stopped crying, but she looked very frightened.

"Please, ma'am. I know that I've been very bad. What are you going to do to me? I'll work extra if you don't fire me. If I have go home, I don't know how I could live it down. Please, ma'am. I try to be a good nurse. It means so much to me."

Miss Mason took both of Rachel's arms by the biceps, lifted her up, gave her a long hug, and gently sat her down again.

"I'm not going to punish you. I just read your nurse's notes. I can't believe how sophisticated you are. You understand the different types of treatments and what the doctors are trying to do. You must have studied and read quite a bit. Very few of our nurses would bother themselves like that. We're also in your debt for being so conscientious about searching the rooms. Without you, we never would have known what was happening."

"Oh thank you, ma'am."

"Well, can you help us with another problem? There's something strange in the way Carrie Adams is being cared for. She's treated exclusively by Shannon Krebs, an attendant, on your shift and Amy Strong, a nurse's aide, on Jane Greene's. Why would Dr. Carson order something like that? They certainly don't seem like the ones that would be the most qualified to work with her. What do you think is happening?"

"I don't know. Dr. Carson's orders usually make more sense."

"Is there anything that ties those two together?"

"It's only gossip, ma'am, but if you think it's important, I'll repeat it."

"Please, Rachel. It's extremely important."

"Many of the girls think that they both go to bed with Thomas."

"Thomas sounds busy. Does he have any other girlfriends?"

"The other names I hear a lot are April Gibbs and Amelia Harrison."

"I know who they are. April's an attendant, and Amelia is a student nurse. When you add Amy and Shannon, the four of them cover all the shifts on the Violent Ward. Consequently, Thomas's menagerie would be enough to isolate Carrie completely. Somebody has manipulated her treatment. For the sake of the hospital I hope that it isn't Dr. Carson."

Suddenly, there were three loud knocks on the door. Miss Mason reacted immediately. She told Rachel and me to stay where we were, opened the door, stepped halfway outside, and heard a quick whisper from someone to her right. She pivoted back to us.

"Quick, you two. We've got to go to Miss Rayburn's suite right away. Hurry!"

As we ran down the corridor, I glanced backward and saw the door to the entry hall closing. When we reached the door to the administrative offices, Sheila was just hurrying up the cross corridor. Miss Mason opened it with her key, then shut it quickly once we were through, and slid a heavy bolt in place. Miss Wells was sitting with some papers and a large mug of coffee at the table in the conference room. She looked up startled, but then quieted down when Miss Mason placed her finger across her lips. Miss Mason then waited for all of our heart rates to return to normal and then pointed to the door of Miss Rayburn's office and made a beckoning sign with her finger. Again, she opened the door with one of her keys, waited while we went through, entered, relocked the door, and shot the heavy dead bolt into place. Miss Wells, Sheila, and Rachel looked a little nervous about being in Miss Rayburn's sanctum uninvited, but Miss Mason tried to reassure them in a low voice.

"Don't worry, please. We should be absolutely safe now that we're behind two locked doors. In addition, this isn't a problem with the patients. They don't know that anything is going on, and I certainly hope they stay that way. Rather, we just found out that a couple of our employees are dangerous criminals who will be coming onto the ward momentarily. The police are laying a trap for them, but they don't want innocent people to get in harm's way. Shush, Molly. It's nothing to do with you, Rachel, or Sheila, but Andy and I could be in real danger. Settle down while I turn on the recording system for Room 23 in case they go there."

I was chivalrous and took one of the hard chairs. Rachel sat next to me, looked at me inquiringly, and when I smiled at her slipped her hand into mine. While we were doing this, Miss Mason fiddled with some controls on a shelf behind Miss Rayburn's desk. We waited for maybe five minutes and then heard the sound of a door opening followed by a curse in a male voice that sounded like Thomas, the nasty attendant.

"Damn it, April. They're gone. There's a nurse's cap here and a pair of panties, but the panties look too small for that uppity bitch. Oh, how I wanted to catch her with her little boy of a nurse."

"Please, Thomas, be quieter. If we're heard, we're the ones who will be in trouble. Don't waste what Amy and I were able to do tonight. They'll both be in jail by Monday morning for the drugs and pornography we planted. Our friend on the Vice Squad is getting a search warrant from Judge Crocker and will be here tomorrow afternoon. I'm proud of thinking to put the bag of cocaine you gave me into the coffee cup Andy used earlier before hiding it behind the strait jackets in the small storeroom."

"Good girl. What did Amy do? Why didn't you tell me what you were up to? I'd have loved to help."

"Amy just did what the Doc told her to. He's the one who gave her the keys to that stuck-up bitch's office. I don't think that anybody knows that she left Brackman. Amelia is going to give her an alibi."

"Well, that might be good enough. I'll make sure that I'm around to see them hauled away tomorrow. I'll bet the uppity bitch will be crying her eyes out and the little twit will be wetting his pants. It's too bad that we didn't catch them with their panties off. It would have been real fun slapping them around while we took them into custody for the drugs you saw him hiding in the storeroom. I'm glad you came to get me when you heard the brat calling her. Come on, let's see if we can still grab them."

We heard the door close. Miss Wells and Sheila looked at the three of us wide-eyed, while Rachel blushed deeply. Miss Mason intuited that they thought that something naughty had occurred in Room 23.

"I see you're suspicious, Molly. What happened was that Rachel found a pornographic magazine and a pair of panties hidden in Room 23 when she did a security check at the end of her shift. Initially, she had planned to report it to Miss Rayburn tomorrow morning at Brackman, which is why she didn't say anything to you at the shift change. However, she had second thoughts and came back where she ran into Andy, who told her that I was concerned about people planting contraband in the hospital. They decided to call me, and I contacted Clem and the detectives who have been investigating Elm Hill. I don't know the details, but while I was examining Room 23 with Rachel and Andy, the police saw some suspicious activity. Then, Detective Perkins ordered us to come here for our own safety."

"Yes, ma'am. I am scared now. That Thomas is awful. What will happen?"

"Let's hope they get arrested. The tape that we just recorded should be enough to put them away for a while."

We then heard three loud thumps on the outer door. Miss Mason let out a sigh of relief and smiled.

"That's the signal. Let's go see what the police have found."

When she opened the front door, Detective Perkins was there. "We found two of your employees acting very suspiciously and carrying knives. They couldn't explain what they were doing, so we placed them under arrest. We identified them as Thomas Reeves and April Gibbs. There doesn't seem to be anyone else around, so I think that you're safe."

"Thank you so much, Richard. These are two charge nurses for this Violent Ward, Molly Wells and Rachel Weiss, as well as an attendant Sheila Mills. I think we have something for you if you'll come into the inner office. We were able to tape a very incriminating conversation in one of the cells."

We heard rapid footsteps. Laura darted through the doorway, holding a single piece of paper and looking excited. "Miss Mason, I just found this in April's purse. If I read it correctly, it looks like Carrie is going to get an electro-shock tomorrow morning at 6 a.m. Can that be right?"

"That's bizarre. Let me look at it. Dr. Rydberg has forbidden electro-shock for her. It would never be performed on the weekend and definitely not that early in the morning. Furthermore, an attendant like April would never be involved, only experienced nurses are. Oh, my lord. I can't believe it. It's an order for April to serve on the team administering an electro-shock to Carrie. It's from Helen Garson, Dr. Carson's administrative nurse. She organizes the electro-shocks for him, but this is totally irregular.

"Well, come in both of you and listen to what Thomas and April say they were up to. I'll think you'll find it interesting."

The tape did indeed perk Detective Perkins up. "Well, this is quite nice, Carol. I think that we're well on the way to sending both of those sleaze balls to the state pen for a few years. After what Thomas did to Emma, I'll be delighted to put him where he belongs. Maybe, we can squeeze him, and get him to sing."

"Well, good luck with that. Also, what should we do about their contraband?"

"Well, we'll see if they'll confess to what they planted. Even if they do, you'll probably have to have an extensive search to make sure that everything's found. Don't worry about a search warrant, however. My friend on Vice will make sure that nothing happens."

"Richard, could you get Matt and Clem for a minute before you haul your prisoners off? I've got a quick question for you all. Please stay, Laura. I take it that you've got April all ready for Matron Butler if she's on duty tonight."

Laura giggled and said she wasn't sure. Then, Miss Mason asked Mrs. Wells, Sheila, and Rachel to wait outside at the nurses' station. When the three men returned, she gave us each a piece of paper.

"Well, in murder mysteries, the one smart detective assembles all the suspects and announces the killer. Here, it seems likely that the Doc is the guy in charge. I thought we could have a little contest. Why doesn't each of us write down who we think will show up to preside over the electro-shock? Sign your name. In four hours we can see who the Hercule Poirot of Osloville is."

She collected the papers and smiled, "Three for Dr. Carson, one for Miss Rayburn, one for Dr. Carmichael, and one for Dr. Rydberg. I see that nobody thought that Dr. Matthews was going to sneak out of Osloville Jail to run the electro-shock."

Once the others left, Miss Mason posted Sheila by the side exit and me by the main exit. She said that she would put signs on the doors saying that entrance was prohibited until the morning shift came on duty. If anyone tried to get in, we shouldn't even wait to see who they were but just run to the nurses' station and push the alarm button.

Chapter 27 ~ Electroshock

Miss Mason returned a few minutes before five o'clock with a nurse who I vaguely remembered seeing around Brackman. The woman replaced me on watch. Then, Miss Mason and I walked out the front entrance on our way to the electro-shock rooms.

"Well, Andy. I don't know what to expect here, but I have my suspicions. By the way, I took Rachel back to my room and let her sleep there so she wouldn't be disturbed. The poor girl had a very traumatic evening. I saw she was holding hands with you. I hope you aren't going to try to take her away from us."

"No, of course not. I was just comforting her. I felt guilty about the way I treated her. When I saw her with that magazine, I thought that she was as bad as Amy."

We turned the corner toward the electro-shock area and saw that Laura was waiting for us. She looked imposing in her uniform and was wearing her belt with a holstered gun and handcuffs attached. Miss Mason let us into the waiting room and told us to sit on a wooden bench along the far wall. She went through a door to the electro-shock theatre, came back after a couple of minutes, and told us to keep silent until something happened so we wouldn't scare the suspects away. At about 5:20 the door to the corridor opened. Mrs. Garson stepped into the room and gave a small shriek at seeing us. She was wearing a starched white uniform but, somewhat incongruously, black rubber gloves and rubber boots.

Miss Mason expressed some incredulity. "Hello, Helen. Shut the door please. Now, why in the world are you wearing boots and gloves? I've never seen such protective wear for an electro-shock before."

"Please, ma'am. Doctor Carson told me to. He said it was a new precaution because there had been some problems at Downsville. I'm the one who pulls the switch for the shock."

"Whenever did he tell you that? Don't lie to me. I'll call him on the phone to check up."

"He left a memo on my desk late Friday afternoon. He told me to arrange this session."

"Well, that's very nice. Have you had so many electro-shocks yourself that your memory was destroyed? You received a direct written order from Dr. Rydberg forbidding you from shocking Miss Adams. I called him at two o'clock this morning. He confirmed that the order is still in place and did not sound pleased with you at all. Where is this memo? You better be able to produce it. You can't, can you?"

"No, ma'am. I left it on my desk when I left Friday evening, but it was gone when I got here a few minutes ago."

"Another thing. How could you have an attendant like April Griggs be involved in an electro-shock? That's a duty for a nurse."

"I just did what Dr. Carson ordered in his memo."

"Well, let's just hope that he shows up in half an hour and says that you're his good little girl. If he doesn't, Dr. Rydberg will take care of you. Now, are you willing to tell us the truth?"

"Please, ma'am. I know you hate me because I'm loyal to Dr. Carson. I'd never do anything like this on my own. I'm not like you. I respect doctors."

"Really, Helen. I'd never expect you to do something crazy like this, but Dr. Carson certainly isn't crazy either.

"Now, let's do an experiment. Take us into the next room and show us how you administer a shock. I've set it up for you, and you're obviously well protected with your boots and gloves."

We all went into the electro-shock theatre, though Laura positioned herself by the door so that nobody could come up on us unaware through the waiting room. Somebody, presumably Miss Mason, had attached the electrodes from the machine to a cloth ball that was approximately the size of a human head. Mrs. Garson walked to the machine at the head of the bed and turned to Miss Mason.

"Dr. Carson calibrates the strength of the shock very carefully, and, when he's ready, I push the switch to administer the shock. It's all straightforward."

"Do you know what the normal strength is? Can you check the setting now?"

"I'm not qualified to do it, so I can't be sure, but it looks like it's in the right range."

"Okay. Please show us what you normally do."

So far, Mrs. Garson seemed at ease and comfortable, but the thought struck me that she was like Melinda when Laura was questioning her about Elm Hill's account with First National. She pressed the switch confidently and then screamed when there was a loud crack, a flash like a streak of lightning, and a burning smell from the ball between the electrodes.

We stood stunned for a minute before Miss Mason's accusing tone broke the momentary silence.

"Were you planning to kill Carrie? That's what you would have done. No wonder you needed rubber gloves and boots."

Laura darted across the room and grabbed the stricken and unresisting nurse by the right bicep. "Helen Garson, I'm arresting you on suspicion of attempted murder. Turn around. At least your gloves will pad your wrists from the handcuffs. Andy, take her to the vacant cell just inside the Violent Ward. She can be confined there until we find out who else shows up."

As we moved through the waiting room, Mrs. Garson begged, "Please bring my purse."

I didn't see any harm, so I did. As we entered the Violent Ward, the nurse guarding the door gasped but didn't say anything. I got her in the cell and sat her on the chair. Laura hadn't said anything about her handcuffs. In any case, I didn't have a key. I suddenly worried about her handbag.

"Helen, I'm sorry, but I can't leave your purse in here with you alone, even though you're restrained. You've just been charged with a horrible crime. I don't know what you're capable of plotting or doing."

"I understand. What I wanted were the pictures of my babies and my husband. I'm so afraid I'm going to lose them now. Joseph is good with them, but he won't know what to do."

I found a little leather folder with her family pictures and laid them out across the top of the table.

"You sound like you're guilty. How could you do such a thing?"

"I'm not guilty, of course. Nurses care for people and try to make them better. But I can't understand what's happening. I know I look guilty."

"Don't give up, Helen. Melinda got in trouble over a forged memo but was proved innocent. We know that someone was in the administrative suite using stolen keys tonight, so there's a plausible reason for the memo to disappear. In half an hour, it all might be cleared up."

I left her looking at her daughter, son, and husband and crying softly. Somehow, it was almost impossible to think of her as a would-be murderess. I got back to the electro-shock suite at about 5:40 and breathed a sigh of relief when I didn't see anybody in the corridor.

As I stepped into the room, someone grabbed me and twisted my right arm behind me. I was pushed to my knees. Before I could regain my senses, one hand forced my mouth open, while another set of hands pulled a rubber gag tightly around my head. Next, a rolling stretcher was pulled next to me. Two sets of arms yanked me up onto it and quickly strapped me down. My wrists and ankles were locked in cuffs to the cart, and heavy straps were buckled across my chest and thighs. I looked up to see two tall women in nurses' aide pinafores, with their heads and faces covered by bathing caps and surgeons' masks. One's identity was quickly revealed, though, when the nearest began to gloat in the voice of Amy Strong.

"Well, Andy. How do you like being manhandled by your supposed friend Helga and me? Look to your left. Yes, we got that uppity bitch of a nurse strapped up, too, like a chicken waiting to have its neck wrung. You shouldn't have come looking for her, like a lost frightened puppy dog. We hope the Doc lets us play with both of you while he figures out how to keep to his plan of putting the blame for frying Carrie on that stuck-up Helen Garson."

I looked to my left and saw Miss Mason strapped to another gurney. I was in shock, especially at the thought that Helga was willing to be a murderess, but I still had hope. Where was Laura? If she had come to harm, Amy should be boasting with glee. Also, Detectives Perkins and Kempton knew about the six o'clock electro-shock. Why weren't the police here? Where was Clem? I couldn't see Clem allowing Miss Mason to face danger without his protection. I only had a few minutes to stew before the door opened again and an unfamiliar male voice boomed.

"Girls, girls. What have you got for me? And, who's my second delectable tall assistant?"

Amy stepped away from my stretcher and responded. "Hi, Dr. Carmichael. That uppity bitch of a Head Nurse and her little plaything showed up, so we got them secured for you. Also, you'll be happy to learn that I talked Helga into joining your devotees. See, she's wearing a rubber apron just to show off her titties for you. She's sorry that she turned shy when you first accosted her. She likes older men and is flattered that a doctor would see anything in her."

"Does she know what we're going to do?"

"She knows that Carrie has to have an electro-shock. I think she'll get a thrill to see what happens. She's excited about the orgy afterwards. I told her a lot about what you and Thomas can do for a woman."

"Where are the others? I take it that Carson's prissy mouse hasn't shown up yet? You better get those two out of sight into the recovery room. We're going to have real problems if we can't pin the electrocution on the nitwit. I'll have a big laugh if she gets fried in the electric chair. I think I'm pretty smart for finding a fall girl for the murders of first the father and then the daughter."

"I haven't seen any sign of Kiss Ass Helen. I'm sure that Thomas and April will roll in Carrie at 6:00 on the dot. Since I recruited Helga, we didn't need Amelia. She's hot in bed, but I'm not sure how she'd handle Carrie's getting zapped. She doesn't know what's going to happen."

"Fine, but get these two out of sight. Thomas and I are going to enjoy raping Miss Mason until she cries to be put out of her misery!"

"Down!"

The harsh women's scream echoed through the room. Amy responded immediately as she went down on her knees and clasped her hands behind her head. The doctor stood frozen with an expression of amazement on his face.

I turned my head to the other side. The other aide, who had been standing by Miss Mason's gurney, now stood with her legs spread and both hands on an unwavering gun that was pointed at Carmichael.

"Down on your belly."

Suddenly, I realized that the harsh commanding voice was Laura's! Then from behind her, I saw the door from the electro-shock theatre open and Detective Perkins walked in. Almost leisurely, he reached under his jacket and drew his own weapon from a shoulder holster.

"Okay, Laura. You can take care of our friends now. I'd be just as happy as you would be to shoot either of these psychopaths if they give me an excuse. Thanks for the confession of the Adams murder, Doc. We've got it on tape. The Chief of Police and State's Attorney will get some dramatic entertainment to accompany their breakfasts today."

Laura holstered her gun. Then she bent over Miss Mason, quickly unstrapped her, and helped her down. She came over to me and began working on my restraints. Even behind her surgeon's mask, I could see a look of near panic in her eyes.

"Oh, Andy. I'm so, so sorry. You shouldn't have had to go through that. Miss Mason and I got separated and didn't know what the other was planning. You shouldn't have been here. I was so stupid. I should have told you to stay safe in the Violent Ward when you took Helen away. I'm so sorry. Once I get you out of these I'll tell you what happened."

After I was free, Laura took my arm and led me to the long bench along the wall of the room. Miss Mason passed us carrying a duffle bag out of the next room which, I presumed, contained strait jackets for Carmichael and Amy.

"When we left the Violent Ward early this morning, Miss Mason and I agreed to meet at the electro-shock suite at five while the men staked out all the ways into the basement. You didn't see her, but Miss Mason had brought Big Bertha with her when she came over from Brackman after you called her. Bertha stopped me on our way out and asked what had happened. When I told her what was on the tape, she suggested that we pick up Amy and her roommate, Amelia Harrison, since Thomas and April had implicated both of them in criminal activity. That sounded like a wonderful idea. Bertha picked up one of your leather restraining belts and a couple of gags from the little storeroom and rode with me while I transported April to jail. As a prisoner, April wasn't very cooperative, so I hope that she tried to resist Dora the Bully, who turned out to be on duty tonight.

"We got back to Brackman about 3:15. We stopped by Miss Mason's room to tell her what was going on, but she wasn't there. I just learned that she had let poor Rachel sleep in her room and gone back to the hospital to check her office. Bertha knew where Amy's and Amelia's room was. Luckily, it wasn't locked, so we were able to tiptoe in, grab them, and gag them before they could get more than half awake. Bertha trussed up Amy in a restraining belt and led her away to the hospital. I handcuffed Amelia. After I put her in my cage, I removed her gag. She turned out to be the opposite of April. She was very frightened and, I'm pretty sure, told me everything she knew, which unfortunately wasn't very much. She kept Carrie from communicating with other people, but she thought that Carrie still had amnesia. As for this morning, she'd been told that she needed to help with an electro-shock because of the special time and that there would be a sex party with Dr. Carmichael and Thomas afterwards.

"I transported Amelia to jail, drove back to Elm Hill, and, as Bertha had instructed me, parked behind the hospital so nobody going into it would see my patrol car. Clem let me into the garage and took me to the recovery room, where Bertha had Amy strapped to a stretcher like you were. The bitch has been in diapers for over three hours. I hope she's soaked by now. Richard, Clem, and Bertha had come up with the idea that Amy should be used as a decoy to elicit incriminating materials from the mastermind. She agreed after Richard told her that he'd make sure that the state wouldn't seek the death penalty for any role that she might have had in the Adams murder. We all thought, by the way, that Helen Garson must be involved. That's why both Miss Mason and I were so mean to her. I'm so sorry for the mix-up."

"Don't be sorry, Laura. Everything worked out wonderfully. He confessed to the Adams murder. That might have been the only way that we could have freed Carrie. You looked so strong when you held them at gunpoint. Somebody said that you're my guardian angel and this morning you were."

She leaned over and kissed my cheek. "Oh, Andy. That makes me happy. Could you please get Helen for me? It's time to get the cuffs off her."

When Mrs. Garson and I returned to the outer room in the electro-shock area, I found that Detective Kempton, Clem, Bertha, and three uniformed police officers had come in during my absence. I took Helen over to Laura. She had removed her cap and mask and was looking radiant.

"I'm sorry, Helen. We thought that all the participants in the electro-shock must be bad. Here, let me unsnap you."

Detective Perkins then coughed and made an announcement with a broad smile. "Earlier this morning, six of us predicted who would be presiding over this nasty affair. I thought that Dr. Rydberg would be the criminal mastermind, so I better make myself scarce around Elm Hill for a while. Only one person singled out Carmichael as the killer. She said that the Matthews case, which has nothing to do with the current crimes, proved that one doctor could forge another's signature or initials because they all write so illegibly. Thus, hats off to our best detective, Miss Carol Mason."

People clapped, laughed, and even cheered. I looked over at the two prisoners, who were standing against the wall in strait jackets and gags. The doctor glared in fury and hatred. Amy's expression was harder to discern, but she didn't look particularly perturbed or psychotic.

Detective Perkins continued, "Miss Mason, I don't feel confident in making a command decision about our prisoners after the fiasco on the night of the Adams murder. Therefore, you can have custody of them until Judge Welch decides whether to have them arrested or committed."

"Thank you, Richard. I'm sure that Dr. Rydberg won't fight you for them. I guarantee that we'll keep them snug and safe for you until Judge Welch lets us know what to do with them. Dr. Carmichael will be our first male patient. We'll keep him locked up tightly in our special security room in the Violent Ward until you want him. Andy, you can have the honor of escorting Miss Strong to Room 23 in the Violent Ward. When you get her strapped to the bed, don't forget to remove her gag."

If the nurse sitting near the door had gawked at the handcuffed Helen, she showed total shock as I paraded the straitjacketed Amy to her cell, though perhaps she didn't recognize her in her rubber cap and gag. When we got into the cell, I removed her gag and cap, laid her down on her back, locked her feet into the ankle restraints, and pinned her body to the bed with three wide straps. As I started to stand up, she said, "Andy, I know you hate me, but please listen. Lean close so I can't be overheard by the monitor. Don't worry. I'm all strapped down. I'm can't even bite you."

I looked down. Her eyes were pleading. I had no reason to trust her, but she certainly was in no position to be a threat, so I leaned down.

"I'm not a good person, but I'm not the totally evil bitch you think I am. You won't believe me, but I like you. You're decent and hardworking and do the best that you can for the patients. I'm sorry I had to be so mean to you.

"I know this sounds bizarre. I'm not asking you to believe it now, but just listen and when things settle down in a few days pass my warning on to Miss Mason. Elm Hill may still be in danger. I'm an undercover policewoman from Chicago. I'm older than I look. I'm twenty-six, not just out of high school. There's a real Amy Strong who's entering Stockholm College this fall, but she doesn't know that I exist. My superiors simply stole her identity for me. My real name is Kitty Goodman, but I'll never be able to use it again because of this fiasco. I'll have to assume a new identity and move a long way away or the mob will kill me.

"I was sent here because of a wiretap that we got in February 1954. The Griggs gang here got ambitious and affiliated itself with one of the major Chicago mobs. Our wiretap recorded a conversation involving Chris Griggs where he talked about infiltrating and then taking over Elm Hill to siphon off the state funds. He mentioned the Violent Ward, but wasn't specific about what he was planning. My superiors got me placed there without too much difficulty. I soon found that Thomas had ties to both the Griggs gang and some crooked local cops, so I let him draw me into his scheme. I think you've found out that they were planning to plant contraband to discredit the good people at the hospital. I'm sure that Amelia will spill her guts about that. Also, I think you've caught most of the people at the hospital. Miss Rayburn, by the way, is totally innocent. She's certainly an old battle axe, but she's devoted to Elm Hill and her ward, even if she thinks your precious Miss Mason is a misguided upstart.

"The one thing I'm mystified about is the Adams murder. Really, until Friday when Carmichael told Thomas and me that Carrie had to be killed to keep her from spreading suspicions, I was like everybody else and thought that she was guilty as sin. I know I don't have any credibility, but I wouldn't have let her be murdered. When my room's searched, I'm sure that they'll find my police automatic in a box that's taped to the bottom of my bed. I was planning to subdue Thomas and April before they could get to Carrie, lock them up, press the alarm button, put Carmichael in a strait jacket if he hadn't run away, and then escape. I'd already called in an SOS Friday night and arranged to be picked up in Swenson Park at 10:00 this morning. I'm sure my handlers will be contacting the hospital before too long.

"There's one thing that you need to pass on to Miss Mason. There's still danger to Elm Hill from the mob. They're working with the Griggs gang obviously, but there's a civic big shot named Mark Reynolds, the owner of Reynolds Construction, who's the driving force behind the plot. Will you tell her?"

"I'll tell her, but I'm not sure how likely she is to believe anything you say."

"I'm not sure if I'd blame her. To stay in character, I've been a horrible person. The way I've acted since I've come here has degraded me. I've hurt innocent people and had to service Thomas and Carmichael. The one thing I most ashamed of is the way I mistreated your friend Jenny Sachs. I was ordered to by my captain, who's a big fan of her ex-husband. Please tell her how sorry I am for her."

"You're right Amy, or Kitty, or whoever you are, it's almost impossible to believe you. I hope your story's true, though. It's hard to imagine such an evil woman as you seem to be. Is there anything I can do for you?"

"Yes, Andy, bend very close so I can whisper. First, please see if Bertha is still around to change my diapers. Second, remember my code name is Bluebird."

Chapter 28 ~ The Day After

Miss Mason walked me back to Brackman. She said that she was afraid that I'd been traumatized and told me that I should take off until Wednesday since I had more than made up for my long weekend. The combination of the long night and my fears and excitement proved effective in sending me into a long sleep. I didn't awake until a little after 5:00 in the afternoon when there was a loud knocking on my door. It turned out to be Clem.

"Hey, Andy. You had quite a night to remember. I've never seen anything like that at Elm Hill. Let's go to dinner. Ella's working late, and Miss Mason has one last show for us at 6:30. Are you feeling okay?"

"I've had quite a sleep. I dropped right off and didn't wake up until I heard your knocking."

As we walked toward the hospital and its cafeteria, Clem passed on another momentous event.

"You'll never believe this, Andy. Early this afternoon, a Chicago police car drove up to the hospital. There was a uniformed driver, a lieutenant in plain clothes, and a nurse who made Dora the Bully look like a beauty queen. I saw them going into Dr. Rydberg's office as I was on my way to see Miss Mason about organizing a thorough search of the hospital. We later learned that they had paperwork identifying Amy as Roberta Harris, an escapee from a high security psychiatric institution for the criminally insane in Illinois. She almost killed her boyfriend by hitting him over the head with a bottle of gin because she thought he was flirting with a barmaid. After she was hospitalized, she half strangled a psychiatric nurse for reasons that nobody could understand.

"Given that history and all the trouble that she's in here, Dr. Rydberg didn't mind relinquishing custody to them. He checked with Chief Richardson and then let them haul her away. They brought their own restraints, trussed her up, and wheel chaired her out. A few of the nurses said some very nasty things to her on the way out. I almost felt sorry for the wicked bitch. If they'd come for her a few days earlier, we would never have been able to nail Carmichael."

I didn't say anything, but actually it made me wonder if Amy's story were true. It would be very hard to believe that she would be caught at the exact time that she claimed her handlers were coming to pick her up. Her credibility leapt in mid-September when I returned to State U. and found a postcard in my mailbox at the Psychology Department. It had a pretty picture of a bluebird on the front, a July 10th postmark from Memphis, and an unsigned message that read, "I really did like you. I miss you, but not Elm Hill."

Evidently, word had not gotten out about the dramatic events in the early morning because the people in the cafeteria were eating and talking normally, which I found more than a little surprising given the rapid flow of gossip at Elm Hill. I suddenly realized that I was ravenously hungry when we got there and went back for seconds, which I normally didn't do. Still, we had time to stroll around the park next to the hospital for twenty minutes before going back to the administrative suite. Clem led me to the little room behind the conference room and turned on the sound system as we settled in to wait for I knew not what. After a few minutes we heard the door to the conference room open, followed momentarily by Detective Perkins' voice.

"I think I'm going to enjoy this, Carol. Ah, that's good that you're putting the belt out of sight on the chair at the far end of the table."

"We've come a long way, Richard. I wouldn't mind if we were wrong on this, but I don't see any way to fault my logic."

After a few more minutes there was a knock at the door, followed by scraping chairs as Detective Perkins and Miss Mason got up to welcome the newcomer. The latter started the conversation.

"Come in, Renee. Thank you so much for bringing our guest through our maze in this suite.

"Hello, Mrs. Adams. Come in, come in. I see Detective Perkins is holding a chair for you. Isn't he chivalrous?"

"Thank you, detective."

"You're certainly welcome ma'am. You must be thrilled to learn that Carrie doesn't seem to be guilty and will be released to you this evening."

"You're right. It's a miracle. I'm so happy and excited."

"Well, I'm happy for both of you ma'am. However, there's one question that we need to clear up before you're reunited with your daughter. Is that all right?"

"Certainly, I'd do anything to help Carrie. What happened, though? Why are you releasing her now? I thought that everyone was 100% certain that she was guilty."

"We seem to have been premature in our presumption of guilt, I'm sorry to say. Early this morning we arrested Dr. Ronald Carmichael and several Elm Hill attendants and nurses' aides as they were carrying out a plan to murder Carrie. During the arrest process, we taped Carmichael claiming responsibility for murdering your husband. After hearing the tape, the Chief of Police and the State's Attorney have agreed to drop charges against her, so Elm Hill has decided to release her immediately. That's wonderful news, but you do see the problem that we have, don't you?"

"No, I have no idea what you're talking about." There seemed to be the start of a quaver in her voice.

"Well, ma'am, there are two things that don't add up, at least in my mind. First, if you hadn't dropped your purse in the driveway, you and Mrs. Ford would have walked up on the porch with your husband, which would have created a real mess for Carmichael. Less suspicious minds than mine might wonder whether you dropped it on purpose. Moreover, you made detailed accusations about your daughter's drug use, but nobody else in your home, the high school, or even the city's drug scene agrees with you. Don't you think that that's a bit suspicious?"

Suddenly, I thought of Miss Mason's enigmatic reference to unrecognized clues after our first meeting with Detective Perkins and felt a thrill that Mrs. Adams' chickens were finally coming home to roost. In fact, I almost laughed out loud at her bristling reaction.

"You impertinent little man. I'll have your badge. And look at that uppity bitch that you've brought in here with you. She doesn't respect doctors. Dr. Carson has demanded that she be fired. Now, I won't talk to you until my lawyer gets here. I'm going to call Chief Richardson, and you'll be out on the street tomorrow morning, if not sitting in a jail cell like you deserve."

Detective Perkins laughed. "Don't bluster, ma'am. It doesn't become you. If you want to go home and get your lawyer, it's fine with me. As soon as you leave the confines of the hospital, I'm going to arrest you on suspicion of murder. You'll be handcuffed, taken to jail, fingerprinted, photographed, strip searched, and put in a striped detention dress. Given the seriousness of the crime, you'll probably have trouble getting bail. Another thing to think about is that if you're convicted, you'll almost certainly get the chair. Your husband was very well loved in Osloville, except by his unfaithful wife and her murderous lover. Trying to frame your own daughter for your crime isn't going to get you any sympathy, I'm sure."

"You bastard. I hate you!"

"Well, ma'am. You sound so refined and ladylike. Listen closely, you've got an alternative, but as soon as you leave the hospital it's gone."

"What is it?"

"You can claim to be a psychopath who needs to be treated for her mental illness. That's how the city's movers and shakers evidently decided to treat Carrie. I doubt that your friend Judge Welch wants to see you fried, but he certainly doesn't hold with killing judges either."

"You bastard."

"Okay, stand up, put your purse on the floor, and clasp your hands behind your head."

We heard a chair scrape as she evidently complied with his commands, but as another chair scraped, she gave one last scream at Miss Mason.

"You uppity bitch. Don't come near me."

Miss Mason's reply was as sweet as her conversation with Carl Roberts when he was taken into custody. "Oh, come now, I know you're frightened, but you need to cooperate. Here, let me slip this belt around your waist. See, that's not bad, and I've already got it locked. There, that's a good girl. Now, we've got your wrists buckled. Okay, now I have to get your leg straps fastened. See, that wasn't too bad. Now, we're ready to go. By the way, I'm taking you to Carrie's old cell. Don't you think that's poetic justice?

Chapter 29 ~ Transcending Gray?

I thought, but was not certain, that the threat of the hospital's being taken over had passed. However, the firestorm of publicity that erupted over the Adams murder kept Elm Hill on the margins. The story told by police and by the city big shots behind the scenes was one of a crime of passion by demented lovers. The two were depicted as psychopaths who had been committed for evaluations that everyone assumed would result in their confinement for life. All their accomplices quickly pleaded guilty to a variety of crimes, but none were charged with being involved in the Judge's murder. As far as the official version went, Amy Strong never existed, perhaps to avoid the embarrassment of explaining who she was and where she had gone. Likewise, the arrests of Kenneth Ward and his two playmates and, a few days later, of Gene Simmons, made the front page of the *Osloville Gazette*, but there wasn't even a hint whatsoever that their misdeeds had any connection to Elm Hill. The official story was that Ward had been arrested for financial improprieties in his parents' Trust Fund at Osloville Bank. What was glaring, at least in view of the evidence that we had recently uncovered, was what was left out. There was no mention of Ward's trying to take over Matthews' embezzlement scheme or of any linkage of Ward's and Simmons' financial transactions at First National to Reynolds Construction, Ernst Reality, or Maverick Motors.

Of course, as the adage "Out of sight, out of mind" suggests, this was no guarantee that that these threats to Elm Hill had vanished. Perhaps, they had even become worse because, since nobody would acknowledge them even after the evidence that we had uncovered, the perpetrators would feel free to pursue their schemes in safety. When I expressed this concern to Miss Mason, she smiled enigmatically.

"At least we know what the threats are. The city's movers and shakers evidently tolerate criminal activity as long as it's kept in the dark and on the margins. However, Elm Hill is so important to the city that letting the dark elements take it over would seem to be an unacceptable challenge to those who think that they're in charge of our civic life. Still, we better keep our fingers crossed since crooked businessmen and the Griggs gang have become bold as brass. Furthermore, Dr. Rydberg and I are not so simple-minded as to believe that a plot to take over the hospital could only involve one member of the Board of Directors, an outside doctor, and a few disgruntled attendants. We still have no idea about who forged Dr. Carson's signature so many times or who got access to several closely held keys.

"Really, Andy, I'm impressed that you saw through the public response of the authorities. Most people here are just relieved that the murder was solved and that the crisis facing the hospital seems to be over."

"I certainly wouldn't have thought like that before I came here. I guess that I was pretty naïve. I just assumed that things were pretty clear cut if you just knew enough to understand them. Now, I understand that the world isn't black and white. Rather, it's pretty ambiguous, messy, and gray."

"Well, you sound like you see the need for Black Angels to try to make things better, even if they can't offer salvation, although maybe it's too bad that they don't make gray rainwear. From what you just said, that would be the appropriate color. What sort of ambiguity do you see here at Elm Hill?"

"The doctors are in charge, but they really don't seem to have much to do with the patients. The patients are disturbed, but they're human beings who deserve the best care that they can get. Most of the nurses seem to understand this, but some of the attendants are actually cruel to them. The nurses shoulder incredible responsibilities, but they're distained and even harassed by some of the doctors. Moreover, there are even rules about their underwear. It's like they're treated as children instead of as the skilled professionals they are."

"Well, I'm certainly glad that you appreciate nurses. There's another thing I want to stress, however. Recognizing grayness shouldn't lead to submitting to it fatalistically. Instead, we need to do everything we can to make things better. I certainly hope that your studies of psychiatric hospitals can turn up ways to improve them. I think that Dr. Rydberg wants to work with Dr. Calder to reform our hospital by showing that there are better ways of doing things. For example, there's a new drug, chlorpromazine, which already shows promise of revolutionizing psychiatric care. On another topic, I realize now that I can't let my personal life drift like it has been. Let's make a pact that you'll come back next summer so that we can work on transcending mental health grayness, hopefully without the distractions of murder and mayhem.

About the Author

Cal is an Emeritus Professor of Political Science at Auburn University. While *The Black Angels* is his first work of fiction, he has authored or edited 25 academic books. He went to college and graduate school in the Midwest, where this mystery is set, and taught in the Rocky Mountain West before moving to Auburn in 1992. He lives in Auburn with Janet, his wife of 47 years. Their favorite activities include keeping up with their three daughters and five grandchildren, hiking, and reading.

Cal is currently working on *A Strait Jacket for Sarah*, a sequel to *The Black Angels* (All Things that Matter Press) that is set two months later, August 1955, at the Elm Hill Psychiatric Hospital for Women.

ALL THINGS THAT MATTER PRESS

FOR MORE INFORMATION ON TITLES AVAILABLE FROM
ALL THINGS THAT MATTER PRESS, GO TO
http://allthingsthatmatterpress.com
or contact us at
allthingsthatmatterpress@gmail.com

**If you enjoyed this book, please post a review on Amazon.com and your favorite social media sites.
Thank you!**

www.ingramcontent.com/pod-product-compliance
Lightning Source LLC
Chambersburg PA
CBHW051119260626
47170CB00005B/1586

* 9 7 8 0 9 9 0 7 1 5 8 9 4 *